The Darkness in Blackwater Ridge

Blackwater Ridge Mystery, Volume 1

Heather Perron

Published by Perron Thomason Publishing, 2025.

Table of Contents

Chapter One...1

Chapter Two..6

Chapter Three 12

Chapter Four 23

Chapter Five 36

Chapter Six 44

Chapter Seven 51

Chapter Eight...59

Chapter Nine...64

Chapter Ten...73

Chapter Eleven...82

Chapter Twelve 91

Chapter Thirteen..100

Chapter Fourteen 112

Chapter Fifteen 121

Chapter Sixteen 133

Chapter Seventeen 142

Chapter Eighteen..152

Chapter Nineteen..161

Chapter Twenty..167

Chapter Twenty-One 174

Dedication

To my Mamaw...

Thank you for always being right beside me, cheering me on and pushing me to fulfill my dreams. I wouldn't be the woman I am today if it weren't for your love, dedication and sacrifice. Thank you for believing in me. I love you!

To my Mama...

I know as a single mom of a heart baby, life wasn't easy. Thank you for always supporting me, loving me and pushing me to do better. You've also sacrificed so much for me and I can never thank you enough. I love you!

To my girls...

I am so proud that I get to be your mom. You are all three doing amazing and are going to go far in life. Thank you for being you. I love you!

And finally to my sweet Andrew...

Being my husband is far from easy, God knows it is. But you handle it well. You're always going along with my crazy ideas, helping me with the animals you didn't want and cheering me on through it all. Thank you for believing in me, for supporting me and most of all for loving me. I couldn't have accomplished any of this without you by my side. I love you forever!

Chapter One

Garrett Cole slumped at his desk, the weight of the last few weeks constricting his chest like a lead blanket. The dim office at the Blackwater Ridge Sheriff's Department felt silent and stifling, the muffled hum of the highway outside the lone reminder of a world still in motion. Boone, his K9 partner, lay by his feet, one ear twitching at faint noises.

The phone on his desk rang, slicing through the stillness. Garrett sighed, rubbing his temples before reaching for the receiver. "Cole," he answered.

"Sheriff, it's Rhodes. We've got another one."

Garrett straightened in his chair, his pulse quickening. "Another what?" he asked, though he already knew the answer.

"Missing woman," Josie Rhodes said, her voice dropping. "Claire Crawford. Twenty-five years old. Her car was found abandoned near Ridgeview Lodge about twenty minutes ago. Same thing as the others. No signs of a struggle. She's just gone."

Garrett closed his eyes, exhaling slowly. First, Sadie Harper. Then Lila Dawson. Now Claire Crawford. Three women in a month, all vanishing into thin air.

"I'll be there in ten," he said, grabbing his keys from the cluttered desk. Boone perked up, sensing the shift in Garrett's mood.

"Ryan's already on-site," Josie added. "We've got the area cordoned off."

"Good. Stay put 'til I get there," Garrett replied. He glanced at Boone. "Come on, boy."

Ben Stockard poked his head into the office just as Garrett was heading for the door. "Heard the call, Sheriff. Want me to come along?"

Garrett nodded. "Yeah, let's go."

The drive to Ridgeview Lodge was silent, the dark forest looming on both sides of the narrow road. Garrett's headlights cut through the thick fog, casting long shadows that seemed to move just out of sight. Driving up to the scene, he tightened his grip on the steering wheel. Ryan's cruiser lights bounced off the trees, making the dark forest look like something out of a nightmare. He spotted Claire Crawford's car on the shoulder of the road, perfectly parked, as if she'd just stepped out to stretch her legs.

Garrett pulled in behind Josie's car, but before he and Boone could step out, she was already approaching, flashlight in hand. Her blonde hair was swept back into a no-nonsense ponytail, and though her uniform was neatly pressed, the worry in her eyes was impossible to miss. "Sheriff," she said, nodding.

Ben stepped out beside Garrett, adjusting his belt. "Damn. Another one?"

"Whadda we have?" Garrett asked.

Ryan Taylor joined them, his hands stuffed in his jacket pockets. "Car's locked. Keys still inside," Ryan said. "Her purse is on the passenger seat, with her phone and wallet untouched. It's like she just vanished."

Garrett's stomach churned. "No signs of a struggle?" he asked.

"None," Josie said. "Same as Sadie and Lila. No footprints, no tire tracks, nothing."

Garrett ambled toward the car, Boone following close behind. He flashed his light through the window, scanning the interior. Claire's purse sat neatly on the seat, her phone's screen dark and silent.

"Who reported it?" Garrett asked, stepping back and turning his attention to the dark woods.

"A passerby. Said they stopped to see if someone needed help but found it like this and called it in," Josie said.

Garrett nodded, his mind racing. "Did he see anything? Anyone?"

"Nothing," Ryan replied. "Said the car was just sitting here like this when he drove up. No sign of her anywhere."

Ben crouched near the driver's side door, examining the ground. "The soil's soft. No sign of footprints, but if she walked into the woods, the underbrush might have covered her tracks."

Garrett scanned the area again, his flashlight beam sweeping over the trees and the road beyond. The Ridge loomed in the distance, dark and foreboding. His gut tightened. "All three women went missing near the Ridge," he said more to himself than the others.

Josie shifted uncomfortably, her eyes darting toward the dark expanse of trees. "You think it's all connected?"

Instead of answering, Garrett crouched next to Boone, who was sniffing the ground near the car. The dog paused, his ears pricking up as he looked toward the forest.

"What is it, boy?" Garrett murmured.

Boone let out a low growl, sending a chill down Garrett's spine.

"Let's expand the search area," Garrett said, standing. "We'll get a team out here at first light to comb the woods. Until then, I want you two to head back to town and start going through Claire's records. Talk to the person who called it in again. See if they remember anything else."

Ben stood, dusting off his hands. "I'll stay here and keep watch—make sure no one tampers with the scene. If anything changes, I'll radio in."

Garrett nodded. "Appreciate it, Ben."

Garrett watched as Josie and Ryan headed back to their vehicles. Then, he took one last look at Claire Crawford's car before turning his gaze to the Ridge.

Something's out there, he thought.

MALLORY CRANE SAT AT the long conference table, absently twirling a pen between her fingers, her gaze drifting over the room. Her boss, Richard Larkin, the Special Agent in Charge, shifted the stack of case files in front of him with a quiet rustle. The team around her chatted in low, murmured tones, the casual banter a stark contrast to her internal focus. The atmosphere was relaxed for the usual Monday briefing on new cases and field assignments, but Mallory's sharp mind was already at work, reading the room.

Larkin cleared his throat. "Alright, everyone, settle down. Let's get started."

Mallory straightened in her seat, placing her pen on the table. She glanced at her teammate, Sarah Kim, who leaned over and whispered, "Think we'll get anything juicy today?"

Mallory smirked. "Hopefully not too juicy. I could use a few days without someone shooting at me."

Larkin lifted the first file and raised an eyebrow. "If you're looking for excitement, you might like this one. Case out of Philly. A string of armored truck robberies. No casualties so far, but these guys are professionals. They're in and out in under three minutes."

Agent David Brooks leaned back in his chair, crossing his arms. "Sounds fun. Let me guess—they're leaving calling cards?"

"Actually, yes," Larkin replied. "Monopoly money replicas with the words 'Banker's Revenge.'"

The room chuckled, and Brooks grinned. "That's my kind of case. Count me in."

Mallory smiled but kept her focus as Larkin moved to the next file. Something about his expression changed—his usual light demeanor sobered, and his tone dropped slightly.

"This next one is different. Three women missing from the same small town in Tennessee. The last woman was reported missing just hours ago. No signs of a struggle, no physical evidence, no witnesses."

Mallory froze. Tennessee. Her home state.

Larkin continued, "The town's Blackwater Ridge. Sheriff Garrett Cole's running the investigation, but they're hitting a wall, so he requested assistance, and given the nature of the case, it has escalated to us."

Mallory's stomach tightened.

"Anything unusual about the area?" Sarah asked, flipping through her notes.

"Depends on what you believe," Larkin said. "The sheriff sounds nuts, if you ask me. He mentions local folklore—Cherokee curses, haunted woods, the works. But we're obviously treating this as a criminal investigation, not a ghost story."

The team chuckled again, but Mallory barely heard them.

"Alright, I need a volunteer," Larkin said, glancing around the table. "Someone to head down there and lend a hand."

"I'll take it." Mallory's voice cut through the room before she even realized she'd spoken.

Larkin looked at her, surprised. "You sure, Crane? It's not exactly your usual beat."

"I'm sure," she said firmly, sitting straighter.

Larkin studied her for a moment, then nodded. "Alright, it's yours. I'll get you the files ASAP."

After the meeting, Mallory returned to her small, tidy office and sat at her desk, staring at her computer screen without seeing it.

A knock at her door startled her, and she looked up to see Larkin leaning against the doorframe, his arms crossed. "Got a minute?"

"Sure," she said, gesturing for him to come in.

He closed the door, put a stack of files on her desk, and sat across from her. "I just wanted to check in. You seemed quick to take this one."

Mallory hesitated. "It's just another case."

Larkin raised an eyebrow. "Is it? Isn't Blackwater Ridge your hometown?"

Mallory's jaw tightened. "Yes, but that doesn't mean I can't handle it."

"I'm not questioning your abilities, Crane," Larkin said gently. "I just want to make sure you're ready. It's different when it's the town you grew up in—especially a small town in the South."

She met his gaze. "I said I can handle it. The case needs someone, and I'm the best choice."

Larkin studied her for a moment, then nodded. "Alright. Just remember, I've got your back if you need it."

"Thanks," she said quietly.

He stood and gave her a smile. "Get some rest. You've got a long drive ahead."

When he left, Mallory leaned back in her chair and exhaled.

Chapter Two

Mallory gripped the steering wheel as her car wound through the narrow mountain road. The late afternoon sun dipped low, forming ominous shadows across the towering pines and oaks, their dark branches twisting into the sky like gnarled fingers. Sunlight filtered through the canopy, casting spots of golden light among the darkness.

She cracked the window, letting the mountain breeze cool her face. The Blackwater Mountains loomed ahead, their jagged peaks bathed in the soft hues of dusk. She tapped the steering wheel, the rhythmic sound assaulting the silence in the car.

As the road curved sharply, Mallory spotted a faded wooden sign: *Welcome to Blackwater Ridge. Population 1,452.* She stared at it as she passed, her chest tightening with a mixture of nostalgia and unease.

She had studied the case file, and now, the names of the missing women ran through her mind: *Sadie Harper, Lila Dawson, Claire Crawford.* When the town came into view, Blackwater Ridge appeared just as she remembered it—stubbornly frozen in time. The cluster of weathered buildings lining Main Street looked like relics of an older, simpler era. Their faded signs swayed gently in the breeze, creaking on chains. The gas station where she'd worked one summer was still there, its rusted pumps leaning at awkward angles like forgotten sentinels. Even the old diner, with its chipped red-and-white paint and flickering neon sign seemed unchanged.

She sighed, pulling into the sheriff's station and parking beside a black truck. For a moment, she just sat there, staring out at the mountains. Finally, she grabbed her bag and stepped out of the car. The air felt cooler now, the breeze carrying the faint smell of smoke from a nearby chimney.

Inside, the sheriff's department was exactly what she expected: small, with a few cluttered desks, a faded bulletin board, and the faint hum of a coffee machine. Mallory approached the front desk, where a young deputy looked up from a computer screen.

"Good morning, I'm Deputy Rhodes," the woman said, her eyes flicking briefly to Mallory's FBI badge. "Can I help you?"

"I'm here to see Sheriff Cole," Mallory replied, her tone brisk but polite.

"Mallory?" a deep voice called out.

Her heart skipped a beat. She'd know that voice anywhere. Somehow, he looked the same as he did when they were young, yet the creases in his eyes spoke of years lived and lessons learned. His dark brown hair, now shorter and more refined than she remembered, bore a touch of gray at the temples.

She stared into his hazel eyes and then glanced at his strong jawline, shadowed by a light stubble. "Garrett," Mallory said softer than she meant to.

For a moment, he studied her, and then a smile tugged at the corner of his lips. "I didn't think I'd ever see you back in Blackwater Ridge. When I heard they were sending you, I was shocked."

She shrugged. "I never thought I'd step foot back in this town either. I never wanted to."

Garret nodded and motioned for her to follow him back to his office. "Just so you know, most of the town isn't happy I called the FBI. People think the women are runaways, but my gut tells me it's much more than that."

"Well, I heard Darla Hensley's the mayor now, so is it the town that's unhappy or just the mayor?" she asked with a sly smile.

Garret chuckled. "Well, Darla's been pretty vocal about not involving 'the feds,' as she put it, but we need help Mal."

Her cheeks flushed at the sound of her nickname. "Well, that's what I'm here for. So, three missing women in a month?"

Garret nodded. "Yeah. All three of 'em went missing out close to the ridge."

"And no evidence at all? Nobody's talking? You have nothing?" she asked.

Garrett clenched his jaw. "No, nothing. It's like they all disappeared without a trace. Poof. Gone. And in this town... well, people don't want to talk. It's worse now than when you lived here. People are scared."

Mallory's eyes widened. "What are they afraid of?"

He stared at her for a moment and then shook his head. "Oh, you know how it is. People are reclusive, whispering gossip and folklore."

As she stared at him, she noticed how tense his jaw was, the way he was tapping his fingers against the counter. "You have any theories?" she asked.

He sighed. "Honestly, I don't have much. I mean, I've got some theories, but they're probably too wild for an FBI agent."

"Garret, if you have theories, I'm all ears. I don't care how crazy you think they may be. I grew up here, remember? I know all the ghost stories, so you're not going to surprise me."

Garrett sat quietly for a moment. "You've been gone a while. Things are different. The forest, the mountains, they're different."

"What do you mean?" she asked.

He ran his fingers through his hair. "I don't know. Odd things have been happening for years—things none of us can explain, and people won't talk about it, at least not openly anyway. Something ominous has settled over the town. I don't know how to explain it. You might think I'm crazy, but I'm starting to believe those rumors about Appalachia curses. I know I probably sound like a damn fool."

Mallory shook her head. "I don't think you're a fool, but I also believe there's a rational, logical explanation for everything, so what odd things have happened?"

Garret dropped his voice lower. "Honestly? It's the woods. Hunters claim to hear strange voices and see things—weird things—especially near the ridge. Most of 'em have started going up towards Knoxville to hunt. And then there's the stuff that's been happening near the old church."

"The church?" Mallory raised an eyebrow. "The spooky one behind the Ridgeview Lodge?"

Garrett nodded. "That's the one."

"That place has always been creepy, but what's happening there?" she asked.

"Odd noises coming from inside the church—humming and singing. Hell, a few people have claimed to see apparitions at night." Then, he held his hand up. "And I know what you're going to say—that it's kids playing pranks, but I'm telling you it's different now. It's weird up there."

"That church has always been weird. What's different about it now?" she asked, her face etched with intrigue.

He shrugged. "I don't know. I've gotta feeling. My gut tells me the church is part of this."

Just then, the door to Garrett's office swung open, and Ben Stockard stepped inside, his gaze shifting between Garrett and Mallory. "Sorry to interrupt, Sheriff," he said. "I just wanted to introduce myself."

Garrett nodded toward Mallory. "Ben, this is Agent Mallory Crane. Mallory, Deputy Ben Stockard."

Ben extended his hand. "Nice to meet you, Agent Crane. Welcome to Blackwater Ridge."

Mallory shook his hand, noting the firm grip. "Thanks. Glad to be here."

Ben offered a small smile. "Hope you don't mind small-town hospitality. We don't get many feds around here."

Mallory smirked. "I think I can handle it."

Ben nodded before turning back to Garrett. "I'll leave you two to it."

As he exited, Mallory glanced back at Garrett. "Seems like a good deputy."

Garrett nodded. "One of the best."

Mallory nodded then sat there for a minute, thinking. "Look," she finally said. "I've been doing this long enough to know that you should trust your gut, but I also know that evidence is what solves cases, so we're not going to get any answers by sitting here. Let's go see the crime scenes."

She stood up and grabbed her bag.

Garret grabbed his keys. "I'll drive." He turned to his K-9. "Come on, Boone."

The dog yawned but stood and followed them out the door.

In his truck, they were silent as they drove toward the edge of town. Mallory stared out the window, her face enshrouded in indifference.

"So... where are you staying while you're in town?" Garret asked awkwardly.

"The Blackwater Ridge Inn," she answered curtly.

"Your mom know you're back?" he asked.

"Nope. I'm not sure how to tell her—or if I *am* going to tell her."

Garret sighed. "Come on. You've gotta tell her. She'll hear about you bein' here before dark. Have y'all stayed in touch?"

"No," she replied. "I haven't spoken to my mother in twenty years."

Garett glanced at her, but they both remained silent for the rest of the drive.

When they pulled off the road in front of the trail leading into the mountain, Boone let out a yip. Garret parked, climbed out of the truck, and let

Boone out behind him. He looked at Mallory. "The car was found just through this path."

"Lead the way."

The path was narrow and overgrown. Long, sharp branches clawed at them as they hiked deeper into the forest. The further up the mountain they climbed, the colder the air grew. The sunlight barely broke through the canopy of trees above. Boone trotted ahead of them, his ears alert.

"It's quiet back here, isn't it?" Garrett asked, glancing over his shoulder at her. "In my opinion, it's way *too* quiet."

Mallory nodded but remained silent.

About half a mile away from the road, Garret pointed out a small clearing, "This is it, right here," he said gruffly.

The uneven ground was covered with broken branches and fallen leaves. In the center of the clearing, Mallory saw the faint outline of where a car had been. There would be no evidence now, washed away by the autumn rains.

"Which woman disappeared here?" Mallory asked.

"Sadie Harper. Her car was found the same day she was reported missing. A hiker called it in," Garrett said, moving into the clearing. "Her keys were still in the ignition, her purse and phone still sitting on the passenger seat. The driver's side door was wide open." He turned to look at Mallory. "It was as if she just turned her car off, opened the door, and walked away."

Mallory crouched and ran her fingers over the ground. It was soft and damp. "There was no evidence other than that? No blood or fingerprints that didn't belong to Sadie?"

Garrett let out a slow breath before he shook his head. "Nothing. No blood, no unknown fingerprints, no other evidence. I'm telling you. It's like she just walked away, disappearing into thin air."

She stood back up, her eyes narrowing as she studied the area around them. "Were there search parties? Did anyone look further into the forest for evidence?" She noticed his eyes darken. "Garret, I'm not saying you didn't do your job. I'm just trying to get clarification."

"Yeah. I got a search party together, but it was only my deputies and a handful of people. Nobody really wanted to come out this far into the forest, but my deputies and I scoured this area for weeks. The only thing we happened upon was a couple of broken branches and some underbrush that may have been disturbed. But then again, this is a forest with wild animals out here, so that wasn't really helpful. If Sadie was here, there's no evidence of it, except her car."

Mallory let out an exasperated breath, crossing her arms. "None of this makes sense. How did her car get here? I don't see an access road anywhere. And how does a grown woman just vanish without a trace?"

"I know it doesn't make any sense. I've been trying to figure this out for a month. That's why I called you," he said, exasperated.

Suddenly, Boone let out a deep, low growl, flattening his ears against his head.

Garrett studied the trees but couldn't see anything, "What is it, Boone? What do you smell?" he asked the dog.

Out of the corner of her eye, Mallory caught a glimpse of movement, but when she turned, she saw nothing.

When she turned back to Garret, he motioned for her to draw her gun. "There's something out there. I can't see it, but I *feel* it. And I trust Boone. He's trained not to growl unless there is a good reason to," he whispered as he withdrew his gun.

"It's probably a damn coyote," Mallory replied, but still, her heart pounded as she withdrew her gun and scanned the trees.

Chapter Three

"I don't see anything," Mallory said. "Maybe it was a deer."

Garret shrugged. "Or a bear."

Mallory glanced at him. "You seemed pretty shaken up a moment ago."

"Nah, I'm fine. I'm sure it's nothin' to worry about."

Then, an eerie sound pierced the silence—a soft, whirring hum.

"Do you hear that?" Garrett whispered.

Mallory nodded, tightening her grip on her gun. "I hear it. What the hell is that?"

Garrett took a small step toward the trees, narrowing his eyes as he focused on the sound. "It sounds like it's coming from the old church," he said, pointing to the path ahead of them.

"Should we check it out?" Mallory asked.

Garrett nodded. "With three missing women, I reckon we better."

As he led Boone and Mallory along the narrow path toward the old church, the hum grew louder, its melody vibrating through the air like a warning. Mallory's stomach churned as the church came into view.

The building looked ancient, its weathered wood peeling away, leaving it bare and splintered in places. The front door hung slightly open, as though someone had just slipped inside.

Garrett stopped at the edge of the path to the church, and his expression tightened. "I don't scare easily," he said with a nervous laugh, "but this place gives me the creeps."

Mallory raised an eyebrow at him. "You're the sheriff. Aren't you supposed to be brave?"

He shot her a half-hearted smirk. "There's brave, and then there's stupid. This place feels wrong—like something evil's here."

Mallory didn't argue. She stepped closer to the church and pulled out her flashlight. The hum had stopped, replaced by an unsettling silence. Boone gave a low whine and turned to look at them, his body tense, his ears cowering.

"See? Even Boone's scared," Garrett said.

"For God's sake, come on," Mallory whispered.

When they reached the church, the floorboards creaked as they stepped inside, the sound echoing through the shadowy space. Garrett swept his flashlight across faded paintings and rows of weathered pews.

Mallory directed her flashlight toward the altar at the front of the church—a simple wooden structure. As she moved closer, unease clawed at her chest, and her heartbeat thundered in her ears.

Garrett's low voice broke the silence. "Mallory, come here. Look at this."

She turned and gasped. On the far wall, half-hidden beneath thick vines, she saw a carved symbol—a circle with a strange shape in the center.

Garrett pulled the vines away. "Look," he said, his voice tinged with nervous excitement.

Mallory stepped closer and examined the carving. It was intricate, a cross with pointed ends surrounded by a circle. A smaller circle and a triangle rested in the middle of the cross. "Do you recognize this?" she whispered.

"Yep." Garrett pulled out his phone and brought up a photo. He held it beside the carving.

Mallory's eyes widened. The symbols were identical.

"I've seen it carved into trees along trails and on old buildings. I did a little research, and this symbol's ancient," Garrett said. "Older than Blackwater Ridge—or this church. "

"What's it mean?" Mallory asked.

But before Garrett could answer, Boone growled low, his fur bristling as he stared at a doorway in the back of the church. His growl turned into a piercing bark, echoing through the silent space.

"Who's there?" Garrett called, his voice sharp, his gun raised.

For a moment, there was only silence. Then a raspy voice whispered, "You shouldn't be here."

A lanky figure emerged from the darkness. The man had wild hair and crazed eyes filled with fear. He clutched an old kerosene lantern, its dim light casting eerie shadows across his face.

Mallory and Garrett aimed their guns at him. "Who are you?" Mallory demanded. "Why are you here?"

The man chuckled. "The question is, why are *you* here?" His smile widened, displaying yellowed teeth. He muttered, "Not safe. Not for you, not for anyone."

"Why's it not safe?" Garrett asked.

The man's eyes flicked toward the carved symbol. "They watch," he whispered. "They always watch."

Mallory asked, "Who watches?"

Ignoring her, the man turned and vanished into the shadows, his lantern's glow fading as he disappeared.

Garrett started toward the doorway, but Mallory grabbed his arm. "I don't think that's a good idea," she said firmly. "We don't know what's back there or who he is, and it's getting dark."

Garrett smiled. "What's wrong? Is the big-bad FBI agent scared?"

"I'm not scared, Garrett. I'm just trying to be cautious. We can come back tomorrow when it's light outside."

Garrett nodded. "I'm just messin' with you. You're right. It's late. We should head back."

By the time they reached the main road, the forest was cloaked in darkness, so they climbed into Garret's truck and made their way back toward the station.

"So that noise... was it that guy humming?" Garret asked.

Mallory shook her head as she stared out the windshield. "I don't think so. No, his voice couldn't carry that far. I don't know what that was," she said, glancing at him.

"It sounded supernatural to me—mystical almost. That's the only way I can describe it."

"I don't believe in the supernatural. Like I said, it was probably a coyote," but her voice cracked as she spoke.

"Whatever you say," Garrett replied.

Back at the station, they climbed out of the truck, and just before they entered the door, Mallory grabbed his arm. "Garret? Before we go in, can I ask you something?"

"Shoot."

"It's not about the case."

"Okay," Garrett said.

She bit her lower lip, looked down at the ground, and clenched her hands together. "Do you think my mom would want to see me?"

Garret studied her for a moment and then gave her a tight nod. "I do. In fact, if she found out you were here and *didn't* go see her, I think it would break her heart more than when you left us."

The word 'us' wasn't lost on Mallory. She cleared her throat. "It's late, and I've had a long day. I think I'm going to call it a night." Raising her gaze to meet his, she said, "I'll meet you here in the morning? What time do you typically get in?"

Garret smirked. "Get in? Darlin', I rarely leave this place."

"Okay. I'll be in at 6 AM. Just so you know, I rarely turn in early when I'm on a case, but uh... well, I better go see my mom. If I don't do it tonight, I'm afraid I'll lose my nerve."

Suddenly, he placed his hands on her shoulders and looked deep into her eyes. Mallory's heart somersaulted. "She'll be happy to see you. Just be honest with her."

"Thanks, Garret. I uh... I probably owe you an explanation, too," she stammered.

He let out a low breath. "Let's solve this case, and then we can talk." He reached for the door, and as she headed toward her car, he called out, "Mallory?"

She turned to look at him.

"It's good to see you again."

ON THE DRIVE TO HER mother's house, Mallory's mind transported her back twenty years ago. She stood at the foot of the staircase, her duffel bag slung over one shoulder and her heart pounding in her chest. The house was silent except for the faint creak of the old floorboards beneath her boots. It was early—so early that the sun had barely started to rise, painting the sky outside the window in soft hues of pink and orange.

Her mother's voice echoed in her mind, sharp and relentless from the night before. "You can't just keep shutting me out, Mallory! I'm your mother, and I'm trying to save you from evil. I know what's best for you!"

The argument had been the same as every other fight since her father's funeral three years earlier. The suffocating rules. The lectures about evil. The endless questions about where she was going, what she was doing, and who she was with.

She stared at the photos on the mantle in the living room. Her parents' wedding picture was front and center, their faces bright with joy. Beside it was a family photo—a summer picnic by the lake—the last one they'd taken before her father's sudden death. At fifteen, she stood between her parents, her dad's arm draped around her shoulder. Her mom's smile had been genuine then, her laughter warm.

That version of her mother felt like a distant memory.

Mallory adjusted the strap of her bag, her eyes stinging with unshed tears. She *had* to leave. If she stayed, she'd lose herself entirely. She couldn't live under Iris' constant watch—the perpetual preaching, the mythical folklore. This house felt like a cage, and she couldn't take it anymore.

She stepped toward the door, her movements slow, deliberate. Her hand hesitated on the doorknob, her fingers trembling. She wasn't just leaving the house—she was leaving the only life she'd known, the town she'd grown up in, and the only family she had left.

"Mallory?"

Her mother's voice, soft and full of sleep, echoed behind her. Mallory froze, her heart thudding painfully in her chest. She turned slowly to see Iris standing at the top of the stairs, her robe pulled tightly around her. Her hair was mussed, and her face was pale in the dim morning light.

"What are you doing?" Iris asked, her voice cracking. "Where are you going?"

Mallory swallowed hard, forcing herself to meet her mother's eyes. "I can't stay here, Mom. I need to leave."

Iris descended the stairs quickly, her steps frantic. "You're not thinking clearly. We can talk about this. Whatever you're upset about, we'll fix it."

"It's not something we can fix," Mallory said, her voice barely above a whisper. "I can't breathe here. You don't trust me. You don't let me live my life. It's too much."

"They got to you, didn't they? Don't go. I can help you expel the evil."

"See? That's what I'm talking about, Mama. You sound crazy, and you're making *me* crazy."

"I'm trying to protect you," Iris snapped, her voice rising. "You're all I have left, Mallory. I can't lose you, too."

"You're not protecting me, Mom," Mallory said, her eyes filling with tears. "You're smothering me. I know you're scared, but I'm not Dad. I'm not going to die."

Iris' face crumpled. "I don't know how to let you go," Iris admitted, her voice breaking. "I don't know how to do this without you."

Mallory set her bag down and stepped closer, taking her mother's hands in her own. "You'll figure it out, Mom. You're stronger than you think. But I need to do this. For me."

Iris shook her head, tears streaming down her cheeks. "If you leave, I don't know if I can forgive you," she whispered.

Mallory's heart shattered, but she nodded. "I hope someday you can."

Iris reached into the pocket of her robe and pulled something out—a delicate silver locket, its chain dangling from her fingers. "Before you go," she said, her voice barely above a whisper. "Take this."

Mallory frowned. "Mom, I—"

"Keep it close. One day you'll understand," Iris insisted. "It's the key to everything. Don't lose it."

Mallory hesitated before slipping it around her neck. The locket was slightly heavier than she expected. She had no idea why her mother was suddenly giving it to her, but she was too emotionally drained to question it.

She picked up her bag, her legs feeling like lead as she turned back to the door. She opened it slowly, the morning air cool against her skin.

"Mallory," Iris called after her, her voice trembling. "Please."

Mallory stopped, her breath hitching.

"Where will you go?"

Still frozen, Mallory remained silent.

"Never mind. Don't tell me. It's safer that way, but don't forget... I love you."

Mallory closed her eyes, her tears finally spilling over. "I love you too, Mom," she whispered, then stepped outside and let the door close behind her.

Mallory shook the memory away, taking a deep breath and staring up at the old, weathered house. The paint was peeling, and the once-bright blue shutters were faded and cracked. The garden her mother had always tended so carefully was overgrown now, weeds choking the flowerbeds. Everything about the house seemed smaller than she remembered.

She knocked lightly on the door, her knuckles brushing the worn wood. For a moment, there was no sound, only the faint rustle of leaves in the breeze. Then, heavy footsteps echoed from inside.

The door creaked open. Iris Crane's once-dark hair was now streaked with silver, pulled back into a loose bun. Her face was lined, her sharp blue eyes still piercing but softer now, as though life had smoothed some of the edges. For a moment, Iris just stared at Mallory, her lips parting in surprise.

"Mallory, you're here," Iris said, her voice low and shaky.

Mallory forced a smile. "Hi, Mom."

Iris stepped back, opening the door wider. "Come in. Don't just stand there like a stranger."

Mallory walked inside, the familiar scent of lavender and old wood hitting her immediately. The house hadn't changed much. The same floral curtains hung in the living room, and the old rocking chair by the window still had the same faded quilt draped over it.

"Sit," Iris said, motioning to the couch. She sat down in the chair across from Mallory, her hands gripping the armrests tightly.

For a moment, neither of them spoke.

"You look... different," Iris finally said. "Older, I guess."

Mallory nodded. "It's been twenty years, Mom. People change."

Iris' lips pressed into a thin line. "Why'd you come back? After all this time?"

Mallory leaned forward, resting her elbows on her knees. "Mom, I'm sorry. I want to fix things. I know I hurt you when I left, but... I needed to go. I couldn't stay here after Dad died. You were so... so overbearing. I couldn't breathe."

Iris' eyes narrowed slightly, but she said nothing, so Mallory continued.

"You lost Dad, and I get it—you were scared. But I lost him, too. I was just a kid, and I needed space to figure out how to deal with it. You didn't give me that. You tried to control everything I did."

"I was trying to protect you," Iris said, her voice trembling. "You were all I had left, Mallory."

"I know that now," Mallory said softly. "But back then, all I saw was a mother who didn't trust me, who wouldn't let me grow up. So, I left. And I'm sorry for that. I should have found another way, but I was just a scared teenager who didn't know how to handle everything."

"Well, that doesn't explain why I haven't heard from you in twenty years. You could've called... could've written. You're telling me that it took you this long to 'handle' things?"

Mallory stared at her hands. "I don't know, Mom. I'm sorry. It's just this town—the mumbo-jumbo... your talk about evil and all that. I just didn't want to hear it."

Iris loosened her grip on the armrests. She looked down, her fingers twisting together. "Believe it or not, I'm actually glad you got out of this town, but that doesn't mean I didn't want to see you—to know how you were doing. I tried to look for you, but I guess you didn't want to be found."

"No. I didn't. I'm sorry, Mom. I really am."

"I was angry for so long—angry at you—angry at myself. I thought you hated me."

"I don't hate you, Mom," Mallory said, her voice breaking slightly. "I never did. I just didn't know how to stay. I didn't want to become like people in this town—rambling about ghouls and goblins, scared to leave, but terrified to stay. But you're right. I should've called you."

"So, what now?" Iris asked.

"I want us to move forward, to have some kind of relationship."

Iris looked up at her, her eyes glistening. "You mean that?"

Mallory nodded. "I do."

They sat in silence for a moment. Finally, Iris whispered, "Thank you. For coming back."

Mallory smiled. "I've got so much to tell you. I'm a cop now. Actually, I work for the FBI."

"The FBI? Are you serious?" Iris asked incredulously.

"Yeah, but there's something else, Mom. I'm working a case—the disappearance of the three women from Blackwater Ridge."

Iris' face immediately hardened. "No."

Mallory blinked. "What?"

"I don't want you working on that case," Iris said, her voice firm.

"Why not? Those women are missing, and someone has to find them. It's my job."

Iris shook her head, her expression tight with worry. "It's not safe. Can't someone else work the case?"

Mallory rolled her eyes. "Let me guess. There's an evil presence that caused these girls to go missing."

"You don't understand. This town, that mountain... there are things you don't know about. Dangerous things."

"Then tell me," Mallory said, leaning closer. "What don't I know? What are you and all the people in this town so afraid of?"

Iris' eyes darted away, her hands trembling. "I can't... I can't explain it. Just trust me, Mallory. Stay away from this case. Stay away from that mountain."

"Mom," Mallory said, her voice rising, "I can't just walk away from this, and if you know something, you need to tell me."

Iris stood abruptly, her hands clenching into fists. "I don't know anything," she snapped. "But I know enough to tell you to leave it alone. Please, Mallory. Don't dig into this."

"Fine," Mallory said, standing as well. "If you don't want to talk to me about it, then that's fine, but I won't stop looking. I can't. I'm sorry."

Iris turned away, her shoulders sagging. "You always were stubborn," she said quietly.

Mallory hesitated, then reached out and gently touched her mother's arm. "I'll be careful. I promise. I wish I could stay longer, but I have an early morning. I'll try to call you tomorrow. Are you going to be okay?"

Iris didn't respond, but as Mallory walked to the door, she heard her mother whisper, "Be safe."

DARLA HENSLEY STORMED into the sheriff's office, her heels clicking on the linoleum floor. She was a striking woman, tall and commanding, with perfectly styled blonde hair and a suit that screamed authority. The moment she entered, Deputy Ryan Taylor, who had been flipping through some paperwork at his desk, looked up and straightened.

"Garret!" Darla's voice cut through the quiet, her tone clipped. "We need to talk."

Garret, who had been hunched over one of the desks in the lobby, looked up slowly. "Darla," he greeted her, his voice neutral but guarded. "What brings you by?"

"Cut the crap," Darla snapped, crossing her arms as she leaned against the doorframe. "I want an update on the missing women, and I want it now." Her eyes flicked briefly to Ryan before returning to Garret. "What have you done so far?"

Garret glanced at the files in front of him. "We're investigating, Darla. We're doing everything we can to find them."

Darla's eyes narrowed. "And yet, you called in the FBI. You don't think we can handle it ourselves?"

Garret's fingers drummed the desk as he looked at her, his expression impassive. "It's a bigger situation than we're used to dealing with. These women didn't just disappear—they were taken, and I need all the resources I can get to find them."

Darla's lips curled into a thin, controlled smile that didn't reach her eyes. "I can't believe you're bringing the feds into my town. Blackwater Ridge has always taken care of its own problems. You don't need to stir things up with outsiders."

Garret leaned back in his chair, his eyes hardening. "With all due respect, Darla, I'll do what I think is necessary. These disappearances... they're connected. Something's off here, and I'm not about to risk another woman going missing just because we're too proud to ask for help."

Darla took a step closer. "I didn't ask for your opinion, Sheriff. I asked for results. The town's already on edge. People are talking. They want answers, and they want 'em fast. If you're too pathetic to solve this case on your own, then you better hope these feds can deliver. But I don't want this to turn into a spectacle. The last thing Blackwater Ridge needs is more outsiders poking around, making us look like a damn circus."

Garret didn't flinch. His gaze was steady, unwavering. "I'm doing my job, Darla. And if the people in this town want answers, I'll get them. No matter how long it takes."

The air between them crackled, a tense silence settling over the room. Darla held his gaze for a moment before she turned and headed for the door. Suddenly, she stopped and looked back at him.

"Just don't forget who you're working for," she warned. "And remember, this is *my* town. You're just passing through."

Chapter Four

The next morning, sunlight poured through the thin curtains of Mallory's room at the Blackwater Ridge Inn, casting golden streaks across the wooden floor. The crisp morning air seeping through the window sharpened her thoughts as she dressed, her mind already occupied with the day ahead—her meeting with Garret, the case, and the nagging questions about her mother.

By the time Mallory pulled into the gravel parking lot of the sheriff's office, the morning sun was high, and the air smelled of pine and dew. She sat in her car for a moment, gripping the steering wheel and thinking about her mother's anxious voice.

What is she so afraid of?

Mallory shook her head and exhaled slowly. She had to focus on the case. Whatever her mother was concealing would have to wait.

Stepping out of the car, Mallory adjusted her jacket and strode toward the sheriff's office. Inside the small lobby, the smell of coffee and aged paper assaulted her. At the front desk, a uniformed officer smiled at her. Donning a neatly pressed uniform, he had short sandy-brown hair and steady hazel eyes.

"Good morning," he said. "How are you this morning, Agent Crane?"

Mallory tilted her head, studying him. She didn't recall meeting him the day before. Extending her hand, she said, "I'm doing well. I'm sorry, I don't think I caught your name."

The man stepped from behind the counter, his smile widening as he took her hand in a firm handshake. "My apologies, Agent. I'm Deputy Ryan Taylor. I saw you yesterday but didn't get a chance to introduce myself. I'm also working on the case of the missing women."

"Nice to meet you, Deputy Taylor. I look forward to working with you."

He nodded. "You can go on back. Garret—or, um, Sheriff Cole—is in his office," he said.

In the sheriff's office, the blinds were tilted, letting slivers of light spill across the cluttered desk where Garret sat with his head in his hands. The tired lines on his face deepened as he looked up at her.

"Rough night or rough morning?" Mallory asked with a small smile, setting her bag on the chair beside the window.

Garret groaned, running a hand over his face. "Rough month, if I'm being honest."

She placed a steaming cup of coffee in front of him.

"You're an angel. Thank you," he said, taking a long sip. "Nothing you need to worry about, but Darla stopped by after you left."

Mallory rolled her eyes. "Let me guess. She didn't come by to tell you what a great job you're doing."

Garret chuckled dryly. "Same old Darla. Sadly, she hasn't changed in twenty years. Actually—scratch that. She's gotten worse."

They both laughed before Mallory's tone turned serious. "Anything new on our missing women?"

Garret shook his head. "No, nothing. I'm at my wits' end. I don't know what else to do."

Before Mallory could respond, Deputy Josie Rhodes popped her head into the room. Her green eyes widened slightly when she saw Mallory. "Oh, sorry, Sheriff Cole," she said quickly.

Garret laughed. "Josie, you can call me Garret in front of Mallory. You know I don't care for formalities."

Josie nodded. "Right. Anyway, I had an idea last night—or maybe it was the Jack Daniels talking—but I think we should talk to Maggie."

"Maggie?" Mallory asked, her brow furrowing. "Who's Maggie?"

"Maggie Whitaker," Garret explained. He turned to Josie. "Why Maggie?"

Josie leaned against the doorframe, her expression thoughtful. "She knows the history of the area better than anyone. And honestly, we're out of leads."

"Maggie Whitaker's still alive? Isn't she nuts?" Mallory asked.

Garret chuckled. "I wouldn't say she's nuts—a bit eccentric, maybe. But you're right, Josie. She's always been obsessed with this town's history, and knowing Maggie, she's probably got some theories on the missing women. Couldn't hurt to talk to her."

Mallory nodded. "I haven't thought about Maggie in years." She stood, slinging her bag over her shoulder. "Garret, would you mind if Josie rode with me?"

Garret shook his head. "Not at all. Josie, you better give Maggie a call and let her know you're coming, though."

"Of course," Josie said with a grin. "Maggie loves company. She'll be thrilled."

As Josie left to make the call, Mallory turned back to Garret. "I'll meet you here after we talk to her," she said.

Garret nodded. "Sounds good. At some point, I'd like to head out to the old church again with Ryan and Josie—extra backup, just in case."

"Sounds like a plan," Mallory replied.

THE DRIVE TO MAGGIE Whitaker's home, a charming old house at the edge of town, led Mallory and Josie through rolling hills and clusters of towering trees. After Mallory pulled into the gravel driveway, she stood in front of the house, noting its impeccable preservation.

Josie whistled, brushing a strand of her blonde hair out of her face. "This place looks like it's straight out of a history book," she remarked, her boots crunching on the gravel as she moved toward the porch.

"Yeah. It's actually beautiful. I don't know why we were afraid of it when we were kids."

Josie laughed. "It's the rumors. People saying Maggie's a witch or a vampire—crazy stuff like that. Like Garrett said, she's eccentric, but she's really sweet."

"Yeah. I remember her. My mom was friends with her."

As they approached the house, Mallory spotted Maggie perched in a wicker chair on the porch. She wore black leggings, and the front of her oversized sweater featured a grinning turquoise cat with sequined whiskers. Sunlight glinted off her neatly styled silver hair. Beside her, a small table held a pitcher of tea and three waiting glasses. She waved warmly at the two women.

"Agent Crane, Deputy Rhodes," Maggie called out. "Come on up! I've made fresh tea, and I have some things I think you'll find interesting."

Her hands tucked into her jacket pockets, Josie climbed the steps. "Nice sweater, Maggie."

Maggie laughed. "Isn't it? They call me the crazy cat lady, so I figured I'd dress the part."

Mallory smiled nervously as she stepped onto the porch. "Hello, Mrs. Whitaker."

Maggie chuckled. "Mallory Crane, well, I'll be damned! It's been, what, twenty years? Your mama called me and said you were back—told me you're with the FBI now. That's something." She waved a hand, dismissively. "And drop the 'Mrs. Whitaker' nonsense. It's Maggie. We're old friends, aren't we?"

Mallory nodded. "Yes. I suppose we are."

Maggie gestured to the empty chairs. "Please, sit. Help yourselves to some tea. A good story always goes down better with a little sweetness."

Mallory settled into a chair on the shaded porch, pouring herself a glass of tea from the sweating pitcher. Beside her, Josie shifted, brushing a strand of blonde hair from her face before taking a sip from her glass.

Maggie folded her hands in her lap, studying Mallory with warm eyes that gleamed with curiosity. "I remember all the talk when you left. Broke your Mama's heart, you know." She reached over, patting Mallory's hand with a touch as light as a breeze. "But you're not here for old gossip. You're here about those poor missing girls, aren't you?"

Mallory nodded. "Yes, ma'am. I was hoping that by learning more about the area's history, we might uncover something to give us a lead," she said earnestly.

Josie nodded in agreement beside her, taking another sip of tea.

Maggie's expression turned thoughtful as her gaze drifted to the distant mountains. "Blackwater Ridge is full of stories—some written in old ledgers and journals, others whispered down through generations. But not many are happy tales. This town," she said, her voice dropping to a near-whisper, "was built on secrets."

Mallory's stomach tightened. "Yeah. Mama doesn't want me working this case. She says there are things I don't know about Blackwater Ridge. Dangerous things. And I get where she's coming from, but she won't tell me anything. Even when I lived here, people were scared, but I don't know what they're afraid of. If I did, it could help us with this case."

Maggie nodded, leaning back in her chair, which creaked on the weathered boards. "Your mama's right. You should listen to her and stay away from this mess. But you're just as stubborn as she is, aren't you?"

Mallory nodded. "Yes, ma'am. So, can you give me an overview? Tell me what people are afraid of?"

Maggie sighed. "Iris is going to pissed. Well, let's see. A long time ago, before the English settlers arrived, the Cherokee called these mountains home. They believed this land was sacred—a place where powerful spirits resided. They spoke of protectors who watched over the forests and mountains, but they also warned of darker forces that lingered in places like Blackwater Ridge. They said the ridge was no place to wander after nightfall."

Josie leaned forward. "What kind of darker forces? Did they ever describe them?"

Maggie nodded, her eyes growing distant as she spoke. "The Cherokee believed the ridge was home to restless spirits—those wronged in life and seeking justice in death. When the Scotch-Irish settlers arrived in the late 1700s, they dismissed the warnings as superstition. But some of the early families, like the Fairchilds, started to believe there might be more truth to the stories than they'd thought."

Mallory straightened in her chair. "The Fairchilds? I've heard that name before, but I can't quite place it."

Maggie's smile was faint, almost wistful. "Yes, they were one of the founding families in the 1760s, pillars of the community for nearly a hundred years. They were deeply religious, so the fact they took the tales seriously should tell you something. But tragedy struck them hard in the mid-1800s. Susannah Fairchild, Hiram and Nora's only daughter, disappeared in 1893. She was just sixteen."

"That's awful. Did they ever find her?" Josie asked.

"No," Maggie said, her voice heavy with sorrow. "She was last seen walking toward the forest at the edge of town. Her father claimed she was heading to see the Reverend at the church, but she never returned. Some believed something in the woods took her, while others whispered that her father might have been involved."

Mallory frowned. "Why would they suspect him?"

Maggie hesitated, her eyes locking on Mallory's. "There were rumors—whispers of witchcraft surrounding the Fairchilds after they began speaking of the legends as truth. Nora Fairchild was said to have come from deeper in the Appalachian Mountains, where such practices weren't unheard of. The townsfolk thought it might've been her influence."

Josie shook her head. "We've all heard about the witchcraft"

Maggie nodded solemnly, then, she smiled. "The kids still think I'm a witch. I *wish* I had some magical powers. Anyway, after Susannah vanished, crops began to fail. Livestock died for no reason, and people reported seeing shadows where none should be. Some claimed Susannah's spirit haunted the ridge, seeking justice."

Mallory's mind raced. "Justice for what? Her disappearance?"

Maggie's gaze softened, her voice lowering. "That's the question, isn't it? Some thought her father might have mistreated her. Others believed she knew something about the town—or the church—that she wasn't supposed to."

The air grew heavier as Mallory processed Maggie's words. There was mention of the church again. What was it about that place?

Maggie leaned forward, her voice taking on a quiet urgency. "There are still families here descended from those who lived during Susannah's time. Misfortune seems to follow some of them, like the Fairchilds."

Mallory's pulse quickened. "What are you saying?"

Maggie gave her a steady look. "I'm saying Susannah Fairchild might not be a distant memory for this town. She might still be watching, waiting for the justice she's sought for over a century."

Mallory exchanged a wide-eyed glance with Josie.

"Are there records on the Fairchilds or the church?" Mallory asked.

Maggie stood, her smile faint but determined. "Who do you think you're talking to?" she asked with a laugh, "I've kept everything I could find. Come inside—I've got something to show you."

SHERIFF GARRET COLE sat back in his chair, the worn leather creaking under his weight as he raked a hand through his dark hair. Beside him, a steaming cup of coffee sat untouched next to a stack of reports.

Near the window, Deputy Ryan Taylor stood with his arms crossed, staring out at the quiet street beyond. His short, sandy-brown hair was neatly combed, but the shadows under his eyes betrayed too many sleepless nights.

He exhaled loudly before turning to Garret. "We've got nothing," Ryan muttered, his voice low but edged with frustration. "It's been weeks, and we're no closer to finding these women than we were on day one."

Garret leaned forward, resting his elbows on the desk. He pressed his fingers against his temples as if trying to ease the weight of the town's fears settling on his shoulders. "I know," he muttered. "But there's gotta be something we're missing. People don't just vanish like this."

Ryan stepped closer, picking up a worn folder from the desk. He flipped it open, revealing grainy photos and hastily scrawled notes. His gaze lingered on the images—bright smiles frozen in time, their faces now ghostly reminders of what was at stake.

"They all disappeared near the ridge," Ryan pointed out, tapping one of the maps in the file. "Different times of day, different circumstances, but that's the one common factor. It has to mean something."

With a furrowed brow, Garret nodded. "The ridge," he muttered. "You know, it's always had its share of stories—ghosts, curses, bad luck. Folks around here believe in that kind of thing." He leaned back in his chair, shaking his head. "But we can't chase legends. We need facts. Solid leads."

Ryan set the folder down with a soft thud, frustration flickering in his expression. "Yeah, but maybe we're looking at this all wrong. What if there's truth to the legends? It's a long shot, and I know she's kinda cooky, but Maggie Whitaker knows all the stories—the legends *and* the history. Maybe we should talk to her."

Garret flashed a knowing smile. "Josie had the same suggestion. She and Mallory went to see Maggie this morning."

The door to Garret's office creaked open, and Ben stepped inside, holding a fresh cup of coffee in each hand. "Figured you two could use a refill," he said, setting one in front of Ryan before handing the other to Garret.

Garret smirked. "Thanks, Ben."

Ben leaned against the desk, his expression serious. "I caught part of that conversation. You're talking about the ridge again?"

Ryan nodded. "Yeah. It's the only connection between all three cases. Every woman disappeared near it."

Ben exhaled, shaking his head. "You know I don't put much stock in town folklore, but something's off about this case. I did another sweep through the reports, checking for anything weird in the weeks leading up to the disappearances. A few weeks before the first disappearance, a couple of hunters filed complaints about strange noises up there. One guy swears he saw lights moving through the trees at night."

Garret frowned. "Lights?"

"Could be nothing, but could be someone up there who shouldn't be. Either way, it's worth checking out." Ben shrugged before turning and going back to his desk.

Ryan blew out a breath and paced the room, his boots thudding softly against the wooden floor. "It's not just about finding out what happened to these women. It's about stopping it from happening again."

Garret stood, his tall frame casting a shadow across the desk as he grabbed his coffee. "You're right. We've got to get to the bottom of this. We owe it to these families—and to this town."

Ryan nodded, his jaw set. "We'll find them. We have to."

MAGGIE LED MALLORY and Josie through the creaking front door, her movements slow but deliberate. Inside, the dim parlor was a maze of overstuffed bookshelves, teetering stacks of newspapers, and antique furniture buried under layers of knickknacks. Heavy curtains, drawn tight, allowed only slivers of sunlight to seep through, casting odd shadows across the room. The air carried the faint scent of lavender, mingling with dust and the musty tang of old paper.

At the far end of the room, a massive wooden chest loomed against the wall. Its dark surface, scarred and weathered, looked as though it had survived generations of secrets.

Maggie ran a hand over the lid, her rings clicking against the worn wood. "This," she said, her voice carrying a hint of pride, "is where I keep the stories of Blackwater Ridge. Journals, letters, ledgers, clippings—pieces of this town's past that most people would rather forget."

Mallory exchanged a glance with Josie before kneeling in front of the chest.

"Not so fast, hon." Maggie wagged a finger, amusement flickering in her eyes. "You don't think I'd leave my treasures unguarded, do you?"

With a dramatic flourish, she pulled a small silver key from her sleeve and turned it in the lock. The lid groaned as it opened, revealing stacks of yellowed papers, leather-bound books, and a bundle of faded photographs tied with a silk ribbon.

"Here," Maggie said, pulling out a worn leather journal from the chest. "I'm not sure who this belonged to, but it talks about Susannah Fairchild and her family. I found it years ago at an estate sale. I tried returning it to the family that sold it, but they didn't want it. Said it was cursed and full of lies. But I've got a nose for history, and something told me this was full of truth."

She placed the journal in Mallory's hands. The leather was cool and supple, the embossed initials—R.B.—worn but still visible. Inside, the pages were brittle, filled with neat, flowing handwriting that had stood the test of time.

Mallory carefully lifted a ribbon marking a page and began to read aloud.

"October 22, 1893. The darkness grows ever stronger, creeping into the very soul of this town. Susannah has seen what she was never meant to witness, and I fear the consequences shall be dire. Should she speak of it, all that we have labored to build will crumble. I pray for the strength to do what must be done, should it come to that."

Mallory looked up at Maggie. "Do you know what this means? Who wrote this?"

Maggie folded her hands and flashed an eerie smile. "Ahhh. I have my theories, but they're just guesses. I couldn't find anyone with the initials R.B. tied to the town. But there *was* a Reverend Silas Bennington around that time. My guess? R.B. stands for Reverend Bennington."

Josie, who had been silent until now, stepped closer, her arms crossed. "Do you think the Reverend had something to do with Susannah's disappearance?"

Maggie nodded. "It's possible. I believe Susannah discovered something about the church—the one *he* founded. As long as I've been alive, that place has been shrouded in darkness."

Mallory carefully closed the journal. "This reverend's church—do you mean the old one outside of town, on the ridge? The one that's been abandoned for ages?"

"That's the one," Maggie confirmed. "It's been empty since the early 1900s, but people still avoid it. Those foolish enough to go near it at night claim to hear voices from the pulpit, even when the doors are shut tight."

A shiver ran through Mallory as she thought of the wild man she and Garrett encountered at the church the night before. She smiled curtly at Maggie. "I think it's awful that this Susannah girl disappeared, and you're right about the church—it's definitely unsettling. But I don't know see how any of this will help us find the women who have gone missing lately."

Maggie's gaze sharpened. "You asked what the people in this town are afraid of, my dear." She held Mallory's stare for a moment before reaching into the chest, pulling out a bundle of letters tied with twine. "There's more. These letters were written by townsfolk in the 1890s, addressed to Reverend Bennington. They talk about strange rituals, missing livestock... even blood sacrifices."

Mallory didn't flinch. "Are you saying the church might've been involved in something evil?"

Maggie closed her eyes. "Whatever happened back then left scars on this town—scars that haven't healed. Maybe someone is trying to finish what was started all those years ago. And if that's the case, the church might hold the answers to stop it."

Mallory let out a slow breath. "Sounds like the church was a front for a cult. It's a stretch to think a cult would survive this long, but it's worth looking into. Josie, I need to go back to the church."

When Maggie opened her eyes, they were glimmering with fear. "Be careful, Mallory. Blackwater Ridge doesn't give up its secrets easily. And sometimes, the truth you find isn't the truth you want."

Maggie's words sounded like something Mallory's mother would say, and she refrained from rolling her eyes. Instead, she offered a polite smile. "I appreciate your concern, Maggie, but with all due respect, I'm an FBI agent. I've handled cases with secrets a lot bigger than anything Blackwater Ridge is hiding." She turned to Josie. "I think we should go."

Josie nodded. "I'm ready when you are." Turning to Maggie, she said, "Thanks again for speaking with us. It was good to see you."

The fear in Maggie's eyes had vanished, replaced by something Mallory couldn't quite define—defiance? Pity?

"You shouldn't be so quick to dismiss Blackwater Ridge's secrets, Mallory." Maggie's voice was steady, but there was something sharp beneath it. "I don't know what you've seen in your career, but I can promise you—this is bigger than anything you've ever experienced. Like I said before, you'd be better off taking your mother's advice and going back to your safe little home up North." She paused, studying Mallory's face. "But I know you won't. So, listen to someone older and wiser than you. Be careful."

Mallory held her gaze, then nodded. "I will. Thank you."

BACK IN THE SUV, MALLORY was seething. "Well, that was a waste of time. She's just as crazy as my mother."

Josie chuckled. "I don't know. I think she's kind of endearing. Besides, she did mention a cult. Like you said, it's worth a shot. We don't have any other leads."

Mallory shot her a sideways glance. "A cult from the 1800s. It's a bullshit theory, but maybe we'll get lucky. I'm not a fan of chasing ghosts."

She grabbed her cell phone and dialed Garret's number. He picked up on the first ring.

"Hey, can you and Ryan meet me and Josie at the church? I think we need to search it again," she said as she backed out of Maggie's drive.

MALLORY PARKED AT THE edge of the forest trail. She and Josie stepped out of the SUV and surveyed the area. The forest felt alive, the rustling of leaves and snapping of twigs warning them to turn back.

Josie moved to stand beside Mallory, flashlight in hand, glancing at the forest with a hint of concern. "Jesus. This place gives me the creeps."

Mallory hesitated, then nodded. "Yeah. I'd rather be busting up a drug ring right now."

Just then, Garret's truck rumbled down the road and parked next to them. He and Ryan hopped out of the truck and walked over to them.

"Alright, we stick together. No one goes off alone. That wild man from yesterday may still be here, so tread lightly. Understood?" Garret said quickly.

As they set off toward the church, the narrow path wound through thick trees, the forest pressing in around them as shadows stretched longer and deeper. The air grew cooler with each step, and the crunch of their boots on the forest floor was the only sound.

Finally, the church appeared, its silhouette stark against the fading sky. In the daylight, it looked even more decrepit than Mallory remembered, its form hunched and forlorn. The steeple leaned awkwardly, and the door hung loosely from its hinges, barely holding on.

"Stay close," Garret barked. "We don't know what we're walking into."

The group stepped inside the church, the air thick with the scent of mildew and decay. Mallory swept her flashlight over the altar, revealing the intricate symbol she and Garrett had found the night before—except now, there was an addition: a phrase etched deeply into the surface.

"They see all."

Suddenly, Mallory's flashlight flickered, and she heard a whisper of movement behind her. She spun around, the beam of her flashlight landing on the corner of the room.

A shadowy figure stood there, mostly hidden in the darkness. "You shouldn't be here," the man from the night before growled, his voice low and angry.

Mallory gripped her flashlight tighter, her hand dropping to the gun holstered at her side. "Who are you? Why are you out here? Do you know anything about the women who've gone missing?"

The man took a large step forward, his face now fully illuminated by the flashlight's beam. His eyes were wild, burning with intensity. "They're not gone. Not really. Not missing. They're sleeping with her now."

"Sleeping? Sleeping with who?" Mallory demanded, her voice rising.

"Susannah," he whispered, his voice ghostly. "She's waiting. And she's not done with this town yet."

Before Mallory could respond, the man turned and vanished into the darkness.

"We need to get out of here," Josie said, her voice shaking.

Ryan nodded. "Agreed."

"No. We need to go after him," Mallory yelled, taking a step forward. "He obviously knows something about the missing women."

Garrett grabbed her shoulder. "No," he said. "We're leaving."

"What the hell, Garrett? We need to get this guy. Bring him in and question him."

"You saw him. He's out of his mind—and he might be dangerous. He's not gonna be any help to us," Garrett continued, his grip tightening on her shoulder to steady her.

Mallory's eyes narrowed. "I don't care if he's crazy. We need to talk to him. He knows something. He might know where the women are."

Garrett stepped in front of her, blocking her path. "I'm not risking your safety—or anyone else's—chasing after some wild man in a creepy old church. You're here to help, but this is still my investigation, Mallory. My call."

Mallory's chest tightened, a flash of frustration flaring in her eyes. "You think I don't know what I'm doing?" she snapped, trying to push past him. "You're letting fear control you. I'm not afraid of some freak in the woods."

Garrett's jaw clenched. "This isn't about fear, Mallory. It's about being smart. You're not in charge here. I am." His voice dropped to a low growl. "And I'm telling you, we're leaving. Now."

Mallory stared at him, a beat of silence hanging between them before she clenched her fists at her sides. "Fine," she said, her voice cold. "But this isn't over. We'll find him again. And when we do, I'm the one asking the questions."

Chapter Five

Garrett's kitchen was dimly lit, the only sound the faint hum of the fridge as the four of them sat around the table. Garrett leaned back in his chair, his arms crossed, his eyes fixed on Mallory.

"I still can't believe that guy just vanished like that," Josie said, shaking her head, trying to make sense of it. "One minute, he's standing there, wild-eyed, and the next... nothing. Just gone."

Mallory frowned. "He didn't vanish. He ran off, and we should've followed him."

Ryan rubbed the back of his neck. "What was it he said? 'They're not gone. Not really. They're sleeping with her now...'"

Mallory sighed. "Yeah. And then he said 'Susannah'—that she was waiting and not done with this town yet."

"So, Susannah's the girl who went missing in the 1800s?" Ryan asked.

"I assume so," Mallory replied. "But it's too convenient. Maggie mentions Susannah, and now this guy does too. I'm starting to wonder if Maggie's more than just a zany old cook. Maybe she's involved in this, too."

Garrett's jaw tightened. "Maggie's harmless. She wouldn't hurt a fly—let alone be involved in those disappearances. But this whole situation... I don't like it. Got a bad feeling about it." He sighed and stood. "Right now, it's all we've got. We need to find out what happened to Susannah Fairchild."

"So, we're going to investigate a disappearance from over a hundred years ago?" Mallory scoffed, standing up and heading for the door. "I don't have time for this."

"Mallory, wait," Josie called, her voice shaking. "Just hang on. Let's at least go over the stuff Maggie gave you."

Mallory hesitated, then turned back. "Fine," she muttered. She reached into her bag and pulled out the old journal, placing it carefully on the table. "Not that I think it'll help, but here. This is a journal from the 1890s. Belonged to someone with the initials 'R.B.' Maggie thinks it's Reverend Silas Bennington's."

Ryan's brow furrowed. "Bennington? He founded the church on Blackwater Ridge, right?"

Josie nodded. "Yep. The journal talks about Susannah Fairchild and how the darkness was growing stronger in the town. It says, 'Should she speak of it, all that we have labored to build will crumble.'"

"So, Susannah was onto something the town didn't want exposed," Garrett said.

"Yes," Mallory replied. "She probably found something connected to the church. But what does this have to do with our case? Who knows if Susannah was killed back then, but she's sure as hell dead now."

"What did Maggie say about it?" Garrett asked.

Mallory rolled her eyes. "She thinks whatever they started back then, with Susannah, might still be linked to what's happening now. The only logical thing I could get from her was that the church was the home of a cult. But how does a cult survive over a hundred years?"

Garrett leaned forward. "Cults can be powerful. They get a psychological grip on people."

"Wait," Ryan interjected, holding up a hand. "How do you know the church was part of a cult?"

Josie answered, "Maggie showed us letters—written by people back then, to Reverend Bennington. They mentioned strange rituals, missing livestock, and blood sacrifices."

Garrett's eyes narrowed. "Blood sacrifices? Sounds like a cult to me."

Mallory exhaled slowly. "The last thing I wanted was to get involved in the crazy, mumbo-jumbo shit in this town. That's why I left. I got so sick of hearing my mom talk about evil and how she needed to protect me."

Garrett put a hand on Mallory's shoulder. "Look, I know this must be hard on you, but right now, it's the only thing that makes sense."

Mallory squinted her eyes and shook her head. "It's fine. You're right. Something obviously happened back then because people here still think this place is cursed. God knows I heard enough of that in high school from my mother."

"So, it all goes back to the church. That's where we start," Ryan added.

Mallory sat back down, still glaring at Garrett. "Yeah. I told you we shouldn't have left. We should've brought that homeless guy in."

"No," Garrett said, his tone firm. "We need more information first. I don't think Maggie's involved, but we need to talk to her again."

MAYOR DARLA HENSLEY stood beside the table in Iris' small kitchen, tapping on the wood.

"Iris," Darla began, her voice smooth, "I'm just worried about Mallory, you know? She's been poking around in places she doesn't belong. It's dangerous, especially for someone who doesn't know the history of this town like we do."

Iris' stomach tightened. "What are you trying to say, Darla?"

Darla leaned in, her tone dropping like she was confiding in an old friend. "Oh, I'm just saying, the town's been through a lot, and Mallory... well, she's a curious one, isn't she? Sometimes curiosity can lead to things you can't take back."

"Mallory's a fighter, Darla," Iris said firmly, her voice steady, despite her racing heart. "She's not scared of old ghost stories."

Darla smiled, but it didn't reach her eyes. "No, I'm sure she isn't. But the problem is, when you stir up old things in a town like this... well, sometimes those things have a way of coming back for you."

Darla straightened and gripped the back of a chair.

"People can get hurt when they meddle where they shouldn't. It's a shame, really. I'd hate to see anything bad happen to Mallory, but you know... there's always that risk, isn't there? And the town... well, it has a way of protecting its secrets."

Iris clenched her fists. "Are you threatening my daughter?"

Darla gave a slow, sympathetic smile. "Oh, Iris, I'm just concerned. Mallory's a part of this town, and I know you want to protect her, but sometimes it's better to walk away before things get too dangerous. You wouldn't want to see her caught up in something she can't get out of, would you?"

Iris' heart pounded. The message was clear. Leave town, or something would happen to Mallory—something that wouldn't be easy to explain.

"I won't let you threaten my family," Iris finally said, her voice sharp now.

Darla donned an expression of concern. "I'm not threatening anyone, Iris. I'm just trying to help you see the bigger picture. You don't want to see your daughter hurt, and I want Mallory to be safe. But if she stays here, well... she might *not* be."

Darla turned to leave, but paused at the door, her back still turned.

"Just think about it, Iris. I'm sure you'll do what's best for her."

IRIS SAT AT THE KITCHEN table, her hands wrapped around a mug of tea. She stared at the phone in front of her, her mind racing. She picked up the phone, her fingers trembling as she dialed Mallory's number. The line rang once, twice, and then, finally, Mallory's voice crackled through the receiver.

"Hey, Mom. Everything okay?" Mallory's voice sounded cheerful, but Iris could hear the exhaustion behind it.

Iris swallowed hard, trying to steady her breathing. "Mallory," she said, her voice low but urgent. "We need to talk. It's about Darla."

There was a pause on the other end of the line, and Iris could almost hear Mallory sitting up straighter. "What about her? Did something happen?"

Iris took a deep breath. "She came by the house today. She's... worried about you. She says you're poking around in places you shouldn't be. But it wasn't just concern, Mallory. It felt like a threat."

A silence stretched between them, and Iris could almost feel Mallory's frown from across town.

"What did she say exactly?" Mallory asked.

Iris closed her eyes, replaying Darla's words in her mind. "She said that if you kept digging into the town's past, things could get dangerous. She said the town has a way of protecting its secrets, and I shouldn't let you go too far. That if you stayed here, something bad could happen."

Mallory was quiet for a long moment, playing with the locket around her neck. "She's threatening me, isn't she?" Mallory finally whispered.

Iris felt a knot tighten in her chest. "Yes. But it's all veiled in this concern for your safety, like she's trying to warn me to make you leave before something happens."

"Mom, you need to be careful. This isn't just about me. Darla's hiding something. I don't trust her."

"I don't either," Iris admitted softly. "But I'm not going to let her run us out of town."

Mallory took a deep breath. "Good. Don't let her. But we need to figure out what she's really up to."

Iris' pulse raced at her daughter's words. "Mallory, are you sure you can't get another agent assigned to this case?"

Mallory sighed. "We've been through this, Mom. I'm not backing down."

"Okay. Be careful. I love you."

"DARLA'S TRYING TO SCARE my mom into making me leave town," Mallory said. "She said some pretty dark things—how I shouldn't be poking around in places I don't belong. That the town has a way of protecting its secrets."

Ryan leaned against the wall, crossing his arms. His jaw tightened. "That's a threat. She's trying to intimidate you."

"I know," Mallory replied. "But why? Do we really think the mayor of this town is involved in any of this?"

Garret raised an eyebrow and leaned forward in his chair. "Crazier things have happened," he said, his voice thoughtful. "And let's be honest—she's been pretty aggressive about this case."

Josie frowned, her eyes narrowing as she considered the situation. "Well, just so you know, her family was one of the founding families of Blackwater Ridge," she said slowly. "Maybe she's just worried we'll make the town look bad. I know she's a pain to deal with and always acts like she's better than everyone, but I don't see her as someone who would hinder the investigation to keep us from finding three missing women. That just doesn't make sense."

Mallory shook her head. "I don't think it's just about saving face, Josie. She told my mom that the town's history can be dangerous—and if I keep digging, I might not make it out unscathed."

Ryan exchanged a glance with Garret, his expression dark. "What do we actually know about her family?"

Garret ran a hand through his hair and sighed. "Honestly? Not much. Her family's been influential here forever. Her dad was the mayor before her, and his dad before that. But beyond their political ties, I don't really know. They've always given me a weird vibe—fake nice, you know?"

Mallory tapped her fingers on the table, her brow furrowed in thought. "We need to dig into her family's past. Something's not right. While Darla herself might not be directly involved, I think she's hiding something. My gut says it's important."

Garret held up a hand, his expression cautious. "I get that we need answers, but we've got to be careful. If we start asking questions about the Hensleys around town, Darla's gonna hear about it. She seems to know what's happening before it even hits the ground."

A slow, sly smile spread across Mallory's face. "Garret, did you forget? I've got resources *she* doesn't have access to." She pulled out her phone and typed out a quick text, her fingers flying across the screen. "Leave the digging to me."

LATER THAT NIGHT, THE door to the sheriff's station opened with a creak. Mallory looked up to see Maggie standing in the doorway, her figure silhouetted against the bright security light just outside the door. She held a large, folded map.

"Thought you two might find this useful," Maggie said as she stepped inside, her boots clicking softly on the wooden floor.

Mallory and Garret exchanged a glance.

"Thanks, Maggie," Mallory said, accepting the map.

Maggie nodded, her eyes flicking to Garret before settling back on Mallory. "It's not much, but I think it might help," she said, taking a step back. "I've been going through some old town records, and this is something I found. It's a map of the ridge, dating back to the early 1900s. I've marked something on it that might be worth looking into."

She pointed to a large scrawled X near the middle of the map. The ridge itself stretched out in jagged lines, marked with landmarks Mallory had come to recognize: the old church, the abandoned mill, and several areas near the creek that ran through the woods.

Mallory leaned in, her fingers brushing over the X. "What is this? A cave?"

Maggie nodded. "That's what I believe. It's been a part of the town's history for years. People used to whisper about it, but no one really ever went near it. They say it's dangerous because that's where the town's darkest secrets are buried."

"Who is they?" Mallory asked.

Maggie smiled. "Oh, you know, just people."

Garret raised an eyebrow. "Why is it on this map if no one goes near it?"

Maggie hesitated, then sighed deeply. "Because the town used to rely on it—back in the days when the church was more than just an abandoned building on the ridge. Whatever happened at that church, the cave has something to do with it."

Mallory looked at the map again. "So, you think there's something down there? Something tied to the disappearances and the church?"

"I do," Maggie said firmly, her eyes narrowing as if she were seeing the past unfold in front of her. "The cave was always shrouded in mystery, but I think it's more than that. I think it's the key to what's been haunting Blackwater Ridge all these years."

Mallory's fingers traced the map again. "Garrett, we need to go there. The missing women might be there."

Maggie's face darkened. "Be careful. I'm telling you this because I want you to have all the information you need, but I can't make any promises about what you'll find. The town has a way of protecting its secrets, Mallory. And sometimes, those secrets don't want to be found."

"Jesus Christ," Mallory replied, her voice rising. "Why do people keep saying that? The town isn't freaking alive."

Garret stepped forward, his eyes focused on the map. "We'll be careful, Maggie. Thank you for bringing this in, and I hate to mention it, but please don't take any sudden trips. We may want to talk to you again real soon."

Maggie laughed. "Me leave? I'll die in Blackwater Ridge, Sheriff. You know that." Her eyes darkened. "Don't say I didn't warn you. There's more history here than you realize, and it's not pretty."

With that, she turned and walked toward the door.

Mallory stared at the map, feeling the weight of Maggie's warning in her chest.

Garret's voice broke the silence. "We'll go tomorrow. Let's get some rest tonight—we'll need it."

Mallory nodded, but her thoughts were already racing. Tomorrow, they would find the cave.

Chapter Six

Garret sat cross-legged on the floor of his living room, going through old books and newspapers that his father had collected. His laptop rested open in his lap, and Boone, his golden retriever, lay nearby, stretched out, snoring peacefully.

"Alright, Rev," Garret muttered to himself, flipping through a stack of local records from the 1890s. "What's your story? Tell me something that can help us."

When Garret flipped through an issue of *The Blackwater Ridge Sentinel* from January 1892, he found an article that caught his eye. He ran his finger over the faded text and read it aloud to himself.

"Reverend Silas Bennington, the venerable and well-respected minister of the Blackwater Ridge Baptist Church, hath announced this week the commencement of the long-anticipated work upon the new church edifice on the ridge. Reverend Bennington, whose sermons are known for their fervency and whose moral character is beyond reproach, hath become a pillar of our community. Yet, whispers have begun to circulate among certain townsfolk, who express concern at the secrecy shrouding the construction of this new house of worship and the true intent of its purpose. Rumors of 'unorthodox practices' have reached the ears of the Sentinel, though none can confirm the veracity of these reports. When questioned on these matters, Reverend Bennington hath declined to speak further, stating only that the new church shall serve as 'a beacon of hope and salvation in these dark and trying times.'"

Garret frowned, his voice curious and low. "Unorthodox practices?"

He turned the page, finding a smaller article tucked beneath a weather report. This one was dated just a month later. Once again, he read it aloud.

"A great and sorrowful tragedy hath befallen the Bennington household. Clara, beloved wife of Reverend Silas Bennington, hath been found dead under most strange and mysterious circumstances. The cause of her passing hath been deemed an unfortunate mishap by the officials of the town; yet the reverend, along with his children—Tobias, Corbin, and Esther—are left to mourn her untimely demise. Whispers among those close to the family suggest that Mrs. Bennington had grown increasingly despondent in the weeks preceding her death. It is reported that she spoke of hearing voices and seeing strange, shadowy figures amidst the woods that lay behind their home. In light of this grievous loss, Reverend Bennington hath requested that the good people of our town respect his family's privacy during this most trying time."

Garret leaned back against the couch, his mind racing. Clara Bennington's death—was it really an accident?

Boone let out a soft whine, and Garret absentmindedly scratched the dog behind the ears. "Hold on, boy," he muttered. "I think we're getting somewhere."

Digging deeper, Garret found an entry in the town's early census records. Silas Bennington arrived in Blackwater Ridge in late 1891, relocating from a small village in Massachusetts, but the footnote caught his attention:

"Silas Bennington hath been relieved of his prior post under most unusual and troubling circumstances. It is whispered that accusations of 'unseemly practices and unapproved rites' were levied against him, though the full details remain unclear."

Garret's eyes widened.

"Strange practices and unapproved rituals? Looks like the good Reverend wasn't quite as squeaky clean as he let on."

He jotted down the information quickly and flipped to another volume—an old handwritten account from a local historian, dated from the early 1900s. The historian described a growing divide in the congregation during the mid-1890s, led by a group of followers who had begun meeting in secret with Bennington. The historian speculated that these meetings likely involved occult practices thinly veiled under the guise of religious devotion.

"Occult practices?" Garret whispered, a chill creeping down his spine.

He stared at the pile of evidence in front of him. Was Silas Bennington involved in the occult? Had he brought something dark and sinister to Blackwater Ridge with him?

THE QUIET BUZZ OF THE sheriff's office phone broke the stillness of the early morning hour. Deputy Ryan Taylor, seated at his desk with his feet propped up on the corner, picked up the receiver, his eyes still on the stack of reports in front of him. He'd been at the station for hours, only sleeping an hour the night before.

"Deputy Taylor," he said, his voice flat.

There was a pause, followed by the sound of someone breathing heavily on the other end. Ryan's brow furrowed.

When the caller spoke, the voice was muffled and low. "You looking for the missing women, Deputy?"

Ryan's pulse quickened. "Who is this?" he demanded, sitting up straighter. "What do you know about the women?"

The voice chuckled softly, but there was no warmth in it. "You're looking in the wrong places. You won't find them where you're looking, but I can point you in the right direction. Head up to the ridge. There's a cave."

Ryan's eyes flickered to the map he kept pinned to the wall above his desk. "A cave? Where's the cave?" he asked.

"That's where they're hiding," the voice continued. "It's not far from where the church sits, on the east side of the ridge. You'll know it when you see it. Just make sure you're not too late."

Before Ryan could respond, the line went dead with a click. He sat frozen for a moment, unsure whether it was a prank or something more serious. Grabbing his phone, Ryan dialed Garret's number, his fingers shaking as he tapped the screen.

The phone rang twice before Garret answered. "Cole."

By the sound of his voice, Ryan knew he woke the sheriff up. "It's Ryan," he said quickly, his voice tense. "I just got a tip—anonymous caller. They said the women aren't far from the ridge, that there's a cave on the east side."

There was a brief silence on the other end.

"A cave?" he said, his voice groggy. "Oh, yeah. We found out about the cave last night. Maggie brought in a map. She marked it. We're planning on going out there tomorrow... or today. Hell, what time is it?"

"Sorry I woke you. It's almost 5 AM."

Garret's cleared his throat. "Alright. I'm getting up. I'll meet you there."

"I'm on my way," Ryan replied, hanging up the phone.

THE AIR FELT THICK and heavy as Mallory, Garret, Josie, and Ryan made their way along the narrow trail to the cave. Boone walked ahead, his nose high, sniffing the air.

The hike was short but steep, the trail winding up the mountainside through thick trees. Garret led the way, his flashlight cutting through the darkness, the beam bouncing off the rough bark of the trees. Behind him, Mallory walked close, her mind racing. Ryan and Josie brought up the rear.

As they approached the cave's entrance, a chill seeped into the air, and a light mist hung in the space between the trees and the rock. Garret's flashlight sliced through the fog, revealing jagged rock walls and the dark mouth of the cave. The temperature dropped even lower as they stepped inside.

"Wow, this place looks like it's been around for centuries," Mallory whispered, her fingers grazing the cold stone walls. "I wonder if this is where Susannah was kept. It's freezing in here."

Garret nodded, his gaze scanning the cave. "Yeah, it feels like a dungeon."

Boone let out a low growl, and his fur stood on end as he moved ahead, his nose working overtime. As they ventured deeper into the cave, the walls grew damp, covered in patches of moss. Faint carvings dotted the rock.

"I don't like this," Ryan muttered, his voice barely above a whisper as he took cautious steps behind Garret. Josie said nothing, but the tight grip on her flashlight betrayed her unease.

They walked further, the silence broken only by their footsteps and Boone's occasional growls. Suddenly, Garret's flashlight flicked over something on the ground. He crouched, squinting to get a better look.

"It's a bracelet," Garret said quietly, holding it up for Mallory to see. "Looks like it's been here a long time."

Mallory stared at the small chain bracelet. "It looks old. It might have been Susannah's. Could prove she was here," she said thoughtfully.

Garret nodded and carefully placed the bracelet in a small evidence bag, his thoughts racing.

As they explored deeper into the cave, they discovered more signs of the past. A torn piece of fabric, possibly from an old dress, lay near the wall. A small wooden carving of a woman's face sat nestled in a crevice. And there were more symbols—some simple, and others intricate.

"Garret, these symbols..." Mallory said, tracing one of the markings. "I'm no expert on this type of thing, but they look like ritual markings."

Garret's expression darkened. "Great. Rituals at the church, and here, too. That's not good."

Suddenly, Boone barked sharply, his voice echoing through the cave. Everyone froze, their eyes snapping toward the back corner, where the dog stood. Garret swept his flashlight over the area, revealing a pile of debris—old and new.

They moved toward it carefully, their footsteps slow and cautious. As they neared, Garret noticed a few modern items mixed in with the old relics—a dented water bottle and a scrap of clothing. Mallory quickly moved forward and bent down to pick up a piece of cloth. She held it up, her face going pale.

"This is part of a jacket," she murmured, her voice tight. "This belongs to Claire. I saw it in her case file. She was wearing it the night she vanished."

Garret leaned over and picked up the water bottle, its plastic still slightly soft from recent use. He examined it closely. "This bottle's recent," he said, his voice tight. "Looks like it's only been here a few weeks."

Mallory's heart raced. "So, all of the missing women have been here. They were kept here... at least at one point. But where are they now? And who's doing this?"

Ryan, who had been silently observing, spoke up. "It's not just about hiding the women. It's about control. And whoever's doing this has been at it for years."

MALLORY GRIPPED THE steering wheel tightly as she navigated the winding, narrow road. Outside, the crisp evening air carried a faint chill, but inside the vehicle, the weight of her thoughts made it feel stifling.

The sharp buzz of her phone on the passenger seat jolted her. She glanced down at the glowing screen, her heart pounding. "Agent Crane," she answered.

"Hey, Mallory, it's Dana," came the familiar voice on the other end.

Relief washed over Mallory. Dana Gaines was the bureau's top technical analyst—a genius when it came to digging up secrets that others couldn't even dream of finding.

"Hey, Dana. Do you have something for me?" Mallory asked, her voice steadier now as she leaned back against the headrest.

There was a pause, and Mallory heard Dana typing on her keyboard in the background. "I'm not sure if what I've found is exactly what you're looking for," Dana began cautiously, "but it's definitely... interesting."

Mallory's chest tightened. "Okay," she said, inhaling deeply. "What did you find?"

As Dana launched into an explanation, Mallory listened intently, her hand gripping the phone like a lifeline. When Dana finished, Mallory sat frozen, the phone still pressed to her ear.

"Thanks, Dana," Mallory said.

Dropping the phone into her lap, she stared blankly at the dashboard. The world outside the car seemed to blur, her pulse roaring in her ears. Her mind raced, replaying Dana's words, trying to make sense of the bombshell she'd just received.

After a long moment, she shook herself from her stupor and opened the car door. The cool air rushed in, biting against her skin, but it did little to clear her swirling thoughts. Mallory straightened her shoulders, closed the door behind her, and headed into the station.

When Mallory stepped into Garret's office, he glanced up from the stack of papers on his desk, offering her a small, familiar smile. It lasted only a second. The moment his eyes met hers, his smile faded.

"Hey," he said, standing quickly, his brow furrowing. His gaze swept over her tense posture, the stiffness in her shoulders, and the way she quietly closed the office door behind her. Something was wrong.

Across the room, Josie and Ryan sat hunched over a table, reading the journal Maggie had given them. Ryan was scribbling notes while Josie traced a line of text with her finger. At the sound of the door closing, Josie looked up, her attention immediately caught by Mallory's pale face and wide eyes. Ryan followed her gaze, setting down his pen.

"Mallory?" Josie asked, her voice tinged with concern.

"Darla Hensley is the great-great-granddaughter of Reverend Samuel Hensley," she said. "He helped Silas Bennington build and run the church on the ridge."

"Wait," Garret said, stepping closer. "You're saying Darla's family was involved in all of this from the start?"

Mallory nodded. "It looks that way. I don't think this is just about the missing women, the cult in the church, or even Bennington. It's about the Hensleys, too. And I have a feeling their history with the town is far darker than anyone realizes."

Chapter Seven

In the sheriff's office, Garrett sat back in his chair and narrowed his eyes as he watched Mallory read from the journal. Josie stood by the window, her arms crossed, her gaze shifting between Mallory and the dark tree line beyond the station. Ryan shifted from foot to foot as if the tension in the room had sparked some kind of anxious energy within him.

Mallory cleared her throat, breaking the uneasy silence that had settled between them. "This entry is from October 3rd, 1893, just a few weeks before Susannah Fairchild disappeared. 'The forest murmurs ever louder with each passing night. Shadows dance where no light ought to reach, and the air grows sharp with a chill that gnaws through even the stoutest wool. I cannot shake the dread that such omens portend ill. The girl has seen more than is wise. She speaks of things best left interred—truths that, if loosed, may sunder all we have wrought. I have cautioned her, and in her eyes, I see that she understands. Fear has taken root, as well it should. Yet the Ridge is not so easily denied. There can be no order without offering.'"

Mallory's voice faltered slightly as she read the last line, the words lingering in the air like a dark omen. She paused, letting the weight of the journal's contents settle over the room.

"Offering?" Ryan was the first to speak, his voice low and skeptical. "What's that supposed to mean? Are we talking about some old superstition?"

Josie, still standing by the window, turned her head to look at him, her eyes sharp and searching. "Or something darker," she murmured, stepping away from the window. "People back then believed in all kinds of rituals, curses, even. Maybe Reverend Bennington wasn't as holy as everyone thought."

Garrett's jaw tightened. "He was a leader in this town. If he'd gone off the rails, wouldn't someone have stopped him?"

Mallory shook her head slowly. "Not if they were afraid of him," she said quietly. "And not if he convinced them he was doing it for their own good."

Garrett frowned, the wheels in his mind turning. "You think this connects to the missing women?"

Mallory nodded slowly. "Three women in a month, all near the Ridge. And then this..." She tapped the page lightly. "'The Ridge is not so easily denied.' He's talking about the same area. It goes with our theory—that the disappearances are part of something ancient."

Ryan scoffed. "What're you saying? The forest is... what? Cursed?"

Mallory closed the journal carefully and looked up at him, her eyes steady. "Of course I don't believe the forest is cursed, but there's a pattern. Bennington's journal, Susannah's disappearance, and now Sadie, Lila, and Claire. Whatever was happening back then, they believed in all this hoo-doo crap, and maybe somebody still believes in it today."

Josie stepped forward, her eyes darkening as she spoke. "There's more," she said, her voice lowering. "I know Maggie's kind of eccentric, but when she was rambling, she mentioned other disappearances—ones that happened decades ago—cases where townsfolk just explained it away as runaways. She said they were spaced out, but they all had ties to the Ridge."

Garrett's hazel eyes darkened with concern. "Well, that had to be before my time. I haven't heard of disappearances like that before our missing girls."

"People don't talk about it," Josie said, her arms crossing tighter over her chest. "Maggie says the older families know something, but they're too scared—or too loyal—to say a word."

Mallory opened the journal again, flipping through the pages covered in the Reverend's neat but increasingly erratic handwriting. She stopped when her fingers landed on an entry dated a week before Susannah's disappearance. Her breath caught in her throat as she began to read.

"'October 15, 1893. The girl has strayed too near to the truth. She speaks of the murmuring in the trees, of the light that wends and flickers beyond the clearing. Worse still, she utters names that were never meant to be spoken. I cannot allow her to bring ruin upon us all. She must be stopped.'"

She looked up at the others, her heart pounding in her chest.

"He's talking about Susannah. She must have known something or seen something that scared him enough to..."

Garrett's voice was low, almost a growl. "To what?"

"To make her disappear." She met Garrett's eyes. "I'm just saying, if Reverend Bennington was willing to sacrifice her for what he thought was the greater good, who's to say someone else isn't doing the same thing now? What if this is all part of some twisted ritual, one that's been passed down for generations?"

Ryan shook his head. "This journal's ancient, and no offense, but it came from Maggie, who isn't necessarily a reliable source. Plus, we don't even know for sure he was talking about Susannah. It could have been anyone."

Garrett leaned back in his chair, his fingers drumming the armrest. "You might be right," he said, his voice thoughtful. "I came across an article the other night about Bennington. It mentioned he had three children. One of them was a girl."

Staring outside, Boone let out a low growl, breaking the quiet and sending a chill through Mallory's spine. Garrett stood immediately, his hand instinctively going to the gun on his hip, his posture tense and alert.

"Whatever's happening in this town," Garrett said, "we need to figure it out. Fast."

ACROSS THE STREET FROM the station, a figure cloaked in black stood in the shadows, watching through the window. His fingers shook as he pulled out his phone and dialed.

"Yeah?" A voice crackled through the line.

"They have a journal. I think it belonged to Reverend Bennington."

"Not to worry. It must've come from Maggie. Doesn't matter. It's not important. She never has anything of value, just thinks she does."

"But what if it's more than that? What if they're getting closer?"

The voice paused, a soft chuckle following. "You're worrying over nothing. That particular journal? It's just old nonsense that came from a crazy old woman. You've got more pressing matters to focus on. Keep an eye on them, but remember—they're not a threat."

"We need to move the women. I'm afraid that journal might give these fools a clue about where to find them."

The voice on the other end of the line let out a long sigh. "I told you. Don't worry about the journal. We've hidden them well. Soon, the Darkness will have its fill. But right now, we need to take care of the other one. Time is running out."

The call ended abruptly.

MALLORY STOOD, STRETCHING her arms above her head, feeling the stiffness in her muscles after hours of pouring over the journal. "It's getting late," she said, turning to the others. "I think we should wrap it up tonight and start fresh in the morning."

Josie yawned, her hand over her mouth as she nodded. "I agree with you. I don't think we're going to figure anything else out tonight."

Ryan sighed, glancing down at the journal. "There's a lot of useful information in here, but I still feel like we're missing something. There's a bigger piece to this puzzle we haven't found yet."

Mallory nodded. "We can tackle it more tomorrow."

Ryan stood and stretched, his joints cracking. "I say tomorrow, the four of us split up. One team needs to go check out that cave again, see if we missed anything. The other team needs to talk to Maggie, see if there's anything else she has that might help. If there's a cult in this town, she's probably the only one who'll give us details."

Josie grabbed her bag and smiled at Mallory and Garret. "I'm game. We'll see you in the morning."

With a final wave, Josie and Ryan made their way out, leaving Mallory and Garret alone in the quiet room. For a moment, neither spoke.

Finally, Garret broke the silence, his voice quieter than usual. "You know, I thought you left because of me."

Mallory's gaze softened, the weight of old memories settling around her like dust. She sat back down at the desk, her fingers brushing the edge of the journal absentmindedly. "I didn't leave because of you, Garret. I would never do that."

He leaned against the wall, his arms crossed as he studied her, a conflicted look crossing his face. "I don't know. You just... disappeared. And I always wondered if it was something I did."

Mallory's eyes dropped to the journal again. "It wasn't you, Garret. It was my mother. She was... unbearable after Dad died. She needed me in a way I just couldn't handle. I couldn't breathe. Every decision I made, every step I took, she was there smothering me. I just needed to get away. I needed space to figure myself out."

"I didn't know it was that bad with your mom. I always thought... well, you just left without a word, and I blamed myself. I should've known you had your reasons."

Mallory smiled weakly, finally meeting his gaze. "I never meant to hurt you, Garret. I just couldn't stay. Not then."

They both sat in silence for a moment. Then, Garret stood up slowly, stretching his legs. "We've both been through a lot, huh?"

Mallory nodded. "Yeah, we have."

"Maybe we can start fixing things now. Maybe we can figure out this case and... maybe us too," Garret said, his voice soft.

Mallory said nothing for a long moment. Finally, she met his eyes, offering a small, tentative smile. "Maybe."

LATER THAT NIGHT, MALLORY sat on the edge of the bed at the Blackwater Ridge Inn, the room dimly lit by the flickering light of the bedside lamp. She stood and moved to the window, pushing aside the heavy curtains. As she stared out the window, she absently played with the locket around her neck. The night was still, the trees beyond the inn swaying slightly in the wind, their bare branches reaching out like skeletal fingers. The moon hung low in the sky, casting long, dark shadows across the ground. Mallory's breath caught when she saw it—a figure standing at the edge of the tree line, partially obscured by the darkness. The silhouette was tall and thin, its form almost blending into the shadows, but there was something unmistakable about it.

Her heart skipped a beat as the figure slowly stepped forward. It looked like a person, but something was wrong. Its movements were unnatural, too smooth, too deliberate. Mallory's stomach tightened, her hand instinctively gripping the windowsill. She leaned closer, trying to get a better look, but suddenly, the figure was gone—vanished into the trees.

A cold chill ran down her spine. She stepped back from the window, her breath shallow. "God, I hate this town," she whispered to herself.

A soft knock at the door startled her. Mallory froze, the hairs on the back of her neck standing up. Her hand shook as she reached for the door handle, but before she could even turn it, another knock came, louder this time. The pressure in her chest grew, and for a moment, she couldn't move.

Then, as quickly as it had started, the knocking stopped. The silence returned, leaving Mallory with nothing but the pounding of her own heart in her ears. She stood there, her hand still on the door handle, staring at the dark wood, unsure if she should open it or run. Slowly, she backed away, her thoughts racing.

Across town, Garret sat alone at his kitchen table when a sharp creak echoed from somewhere upstairs. Garret's eyes snapped up, his muscles tensing. He knew the house wasn't settled yet—it was old, the kind of place where the floors groaned and the pipes moaned—but this sound was different. It wasn't the usual creak of settling wood. It was deliberate, like someone walking across the floor above him. Boone's ears shot up, and he let out a low whine.

The noise came again, closer this time, and then, he heard a soft knock—a slow, rhythmic tap that echoed through the otherwise quiet house. It sounded as though it came from the back door, the one that led to the darkened yard.

Garrett's breath caught, and he stood from his chair, instinctively reaching for the gun he kept in the drawer. Boone growled and moved to the doorway into the kitchen, his hackles raised and his eyes locked on the back door.

The knock came again, louder this time. But Garret didn't move. Finally, he shook his head and whispered to himself, "Get it together."

He slowly walked toward the door, his hand hovering near the knob, but as he reached for it, the knocking stopped, and everything fell into an unnerving silence.

THE SHERIFF'S STATION was quiet when Mallory, Garret, Ryan, and Josie walked through the front door. The early morning light filtered through the blinds, casting long shadows across the dusty floor. Garret's boots echoed on the wood as he walked toward his desk. Ryan, Josie, and Mallory followed closely behind him.

In Garrett's office, Mallory cleared her throat. "I need to tell you all something," Mallory said. "Last night... I saw something outside my window—a figure, standing in the trees near the edge of the inn. I think it was a person, but then again, it moved too smoothly, too deliberately."

Ryan raised an eyebrow, but Josie's gaze sharpened. "What did it look like?"

Mallory hesitated before answering. "It was hard to make out in the dark, but... it was tall, thin. Like a person, but not really. It disappeared as soon as I blinked. I thought maybe my mind was playing tricks, but then there was a knock at my door. Soft at first, then louder. Like someone was waiting for me to answer. It was late, so I didn't open it."

Josie exchanged a quick glance with Ryan, then turned her attention back to Mallory. "So, do you think this is connected to the case?"

Mallory nodded slowly. "Yeah. Look, in the FBI, I've learned to trust my instincts, and whatever that was last night, it felt like a warning. Anyway, you know I don't believe in all the ghost stories, but I do know that something's wrong in this town. I can feel it."

Garret, who had been quiet until now, stepped forward, his expression darkening. "You're not the only one," he said, his voice gravelly. "Last night, after I got home... I heard something. A knock, just like you. At first, I thought it was nothing, just the house settling, but then I heard it again—soft at first, then louder. Like someone was standing at my back door." He paused, his jaw tightening. "I didn't go to check, either. I just... I don't know. I didn't want to."

Ryan leaned against the wall, his arms crossed. "So, what? You both got a knock at your door last night," he said, his voice low and skeptical. "How can that be connected to the case? To the missing women?"

"I don't know," Garret replied. "But it feels like more than just coincidence. There's something in the air around here—something bad."

Josie nodded, stepping closer to the table. "I've been thinking about what Maggie said—about other disappearances, the older ones. She said the Ridge has a way of taking people who get too close to the truth." Her voice dropped lower. "And if we get too close, well..."

Mallory held her hand up. "Whoa. Hold on a minute. Are you suggesting that we'll disappear too? We're not stopping this investigation."

"I'm not saying that," Josie replied. "I was just thinking about the situation as a whole. If people have been disappearing near the Ridge for decades, and the older families know something about it, but maybe they're too afraid to talk. Too loyal. If what we're dealing with is tied to the Ridge... then we're not just looking for one killer or kidnapper. We're looking for something much bigger."

Ryan gave a skeptical grunt. "Something bigger? Yeah. It's a freaking cult that has survived hundreds of years, but I wish y'all would quit acting like this town has a curse on it."

"I agree with Ryan. I've told you before, and I'll say it again. I rely on facts—on evidence. I don't believe in curses or even the supernatural," Mallory said, her voice growing firmer. "Still, I just told you about the knock on my door because I know something is off in this town, and whatever it is, it doesn't want us digging around."

Garret cleared his throat. "Okay. Enough talk. I say we stick to the plan and split up. We can't just keep sitting here and hoping for answers to come to us. We go in pairs like Ryan suggested last night. Mallory, you and Josie go see Maggie while Ryan and I head out to the cave."

Ryan looked from Garret to Mallory, then to Josie. "I know I suggested the cave, but do we really think we missed something the first time?" he asked, his tone cautious.

"What's wrong? You scared?" Josie asked with a chuckle.

"No. I..."

"I think it's worth a shot." Garrett interrupted. "We don't have any other leads right now."

Chapter Eight

The small, cluttered room of Maggie Whitaker's home smelled of aged paper and dust. Mallory and Josie sat across from her at a wooden table, the surface worn smooth by time, surrounded by stacks of old books, papers, and faded photographs.

"Maggie, what can you tell us about Susannah Fairchild and her relationship with Silas Bennington?" Mallory asked.

Maggie's expression tightened as she settled deeper into her chair. Her eyes flickered toward the window, as if searching the darkening landscape for answers. Finally, she exhaled slowly.

"Susannah Fairchild and Silas Bennington's relationship wasn't exactly what people thought it was," Maggie began, her voice low. "The town always believed Susannah was just a sweet, innocent girl, but there were whispers—rumors—about her and Silas' son, Tobias." She paused, glancing at Mallory and Josie. "Supposedly, Tobias was courting her, and Reverend Bennington wasn't happy about it."

Josie's eyes widened. "Was he opposed to it because of Tobias' position as his son?"

Maggie's lips pressed into a thin line. "I think it was more than that. Tobias was... different from his father. He was a bit of a dreamer, not as consumed by the church like his father. He wanted a life of his own, and Susannah was part of that. But Silas? He saw it as a threat, something that could unravel his family's place in the town. And when the rumors about Susannah being pregnant started swirling, that's when everything spiraled out of control. Reverend Bennington didn't want any part of that. He couldn't afford the scandal, especially with his position in the community."

Mallory leaned forward, absorbing every word. "So, Susannah and Tobias were involved? And the Reverend was against it because of the pregnancy?"

Maggie nodded slowly. "That's the thought anyway. Some said Tobias had promised to marry her, but Silas would never let his son marry a girl from a family with such a questionable reputation, especially if she was carrying Tobias' child. It's said that Silas even tried to force Tobias to break it off."

She shifted in her chair, her eyes flickering to the door as if she expected someone to walk in.

"Anyway, two days after Susannah vanished, Tobias was found dead in the woods. They said it was a hunting accident, but I don't believe it. A lot of people thought the Reverend had a hand in it—that Tobias had become too much of a threat, too wild for his father to control."

Josie's voice trembled. "You think the Reverend killed Tobias?"

Maggie's eyes locked onto Josie's with a sharp, knowing look. "I think he was capable of it. Silas Bennington was a powerful man, and he wouldn't have let his son's actions threaten his grip on the town. No one knew what went on behind closed doors, but there were enough whispers to make you wonder."

Mallory's heart beat faster. "And the town, what did they think about it all?"

Maggie's face darkened further. "Some believed that the Reverend had a hand in Tobias' death—and a whole lot more. People whispered about what had been going on at the church, things that were hidden in the shadows. And like I told you before, after Susannah disappeared, crops started to fail, and livestock started dying for no reason. People reported seeing strange things in the woods. Some believed it was a curse, something tied to the Fairchild family's history. But others thought Susannah's spirit was seeking justice. But the Reverend was too powerful to go against, so no one dared to speak up."

Mallory's voice was quiet but insistent. "If they thought Susannah's spirit was seeking justice, does that mean they thought she was murdered?"

Maggie's gaze softened, and she smiled. "I don't know. But I think her spirit wanted to reveal the truth about what happened to her and what her family went through. Some said she knew something about the Reverend or the church that could destroy them all."

"Maggie, I know this all happened a long time ago, but do you think any of this could be connected to what's happening now? With the other disappearances?" Mallory asked.

Maggie stared at her hands, folded tightly in her lap. "I think you're asking the right questions. But be careful, Mallory. The Ridge holds secrets, and some of them should stay buried." She stood up slowly, walking to a shelf lined with worn books. After a moment, she pulled out a book and handed it to Mallory. "This belonged to my grandmother. It might help you. It's not much, but it's something. Take it with you. I don't want to answer any more questions today."

THE AIR WAS THICK WITH the scent of pine and damp earth as Garret and Ryan made their way toward the cave at the base of Blackwater Ridge. The sun had long since sunk behind the mountains, leaving the forest cloaked in shadows that seemed to shift with every step. The trail was narrow and uneven, overgrown with tangled roots and brambles that tugged at their boots.

Garret led the way, his hand resting on the butt of his gun as he scanned the surrounding woods. Ryan followed closely, his flashlight bouncing with each step, cutting through the darkness ahead.

"This place gives me the creeps," Ryan muttered, his voice low. "I swear, it feels like something's watching us."

"We're almost there," Garret said, trying to shake off his own sense of unease. He motioned toward a large rock formation up ahead, where the cave's entrance lay hidden in the shadows.

As they neared the cave, Ryan flicked his flashlight toward the ground, scanning for anything they might have missed earlier.

"This is where we found part of Claire's jacket," Garret said, kneeling by the entrance of the cave. "Let's see if we can figure out what happened here."

Ryan crouched beside him, moving aside rocks and peering into the dark mouth of the cave. He pulled a glove from his pocket and slipped it on, reaching into the narrow opening and pushing aside debris. His flashlight caught on something beneath a large rock, its edges weathered and worn.

"What is that?" he asked himself.

Ryan directed his flashlight to the small area tucked into a corner, concealed by an overhang of jagged stone. He turned over the large rock and froze, his eyes widening as a piece of crumpled paper came into view. He bent closer, his heart quickening.

"Garret, come look at this," Ryan called, his voice tight with unease.

As Garret moved to his side, crouching beside him, Ryan gently handed him the brittle paper. Garret unfolded it carefully and scanned the faded ink.

"It's signed by Susannah," Garret murmured, his brow furrowing.

Ryan swallowed hard. "This definitely gives us proof she was held here, right?"

Garret nodded. "Yeah. If it's authentic." He tucked the paper into his jacket pocket. "This might be the break we need."

Ryan hesitated, looking around the cave once more, his flashlight sweeping the dark corners. The shadows seemed to deepen in response, as though the cave itself was alive.

Suddenly, the air around them shifted, and the temperature dropped. A shadow moved just beyond their vision, a flicker of movement in the corner of the cave.

Garret's eyes narrowed, his hand instinctively resting on his gun. "Did you see that?" he whispered.

Ryan's heart thudded in his chest. "Yeah... What the hell was that?"

The wind outside the cave picked up, howling through the trees, but inside, everything was still. Too still. They both stood motionless, listening to the unsettling silence.

Then, the faintest sound drifted through the air, like a whisper on the wind. It wasn't words, not exactly, but it was something. A hum, a vibration that seemed to reverberate from the stone beneath their feet.

Ryan took a step back, his eyes wide with fear. "What was that?"

Garret didn't answer. He was already moving toward the exit of the cave. "I don't know. An earthquake? An impending rock slide? Whatever it was, we need to get out of here," he said, his voice harsh.

After exiting the cave and returning down the path, Ryan glanced over his shoulder one last time, half-expecting to see something emerge from the cave's darkness. But there was nothing. Just the empty, oppressive silence of the Ridge.

"Let's get out of here," Garret said again, as he scurried down the path.

Neither man spoke until they were safely back on the main road. Finally, Ryan broke the silence. "I don't want to sound crazy, but that sound... that vibration... that wasn't an earthquake. I mean, yeah, we get earthquakes every now and then, but we usually don't even know they happened because they're so minor. That was... I don't know... something else."

Garrett sighed. "I know what you're getting at, and I agree with you. Something felt off, but I'm trying to be logical about all this. I can't arrest a damn ghost." Just then, Garret's phone buzzed. "This is Cole," he answered, and then, his face instantly drained of color.

"What?" Ryan asked, noticing Garrett's expression.

"On the way," he muttered, ending the call abruptly. Garrett turned to Ryan, and said, "We've got another missing woman."

Chapter Nine

The drive to Ridgeview Lodge was heavy with tension and silence. Boone sat alert in the backseat. Ryan stared out the passenger window, lost in thought. Garret's knuckles were white as he gripped the steering wheel, his jaw clenched tightly in grim determination.

As they turned onto the gravel path leading to the lodge, Ryan asked, "Do we have a name on the missing woman?"

Garret's eyes flickered briefly toward him, then back to the road. "Ben didn't give me much other than another disappearance."

Ryan sighed, rubbing a hand over his face. "We need to figure this out before someone else gets hurt," he muttered.

At the Lodge, Deputy Ben Stockard was already waiting for them. He stood just outside the entrance, his wide-brimmed hat pulled low over his eyes, his expression somber and tense. He waved them over as they got out of the vehicle.

"Sheriff Cole, Deputy Taylor," he greeted them, his voice grave as he motioned toward the building. "The missing woman's name is Natalie Baxter. She's a college student from Knoxville, here working a summer job at the lodge. When she didn't show up for her evening shift, the owner tried calling her but got no answer. He found her car in the parking lot, but no sign of Natalie. He called it in after he did a small search around the lodge."

"Any signs of a struggle around her car?" Garret asked.

Ben shook his head, grim. "No. The owner's been through everything. The driver's door was open, her uniform was in the backseat, and her purse was beside it. No sign of her. He checked the security cameras, but they were disabled. Last footage we have is from yesterday afternoon."

Ryan frowned. "How did he not notice the cameras were down for over twenty-four hours? Does Natalie have any ties to the other missing women?"

Ben looked apologetic. "I don't know, Deputy Taylor. We only got the call right before I reached out to you. I haven't had time to dig into her background yet."

Just as Garret was about to speak again, a familiar black SUV pulled into the parking lot. Mallory scanned the scene as she got out, her posture straight and determined. Josie followed her.

"We're here," Mallory said as she approached the group. She gave Garret a quick nod before turning to Ben. "Where's the car?"

"Right over here," Ben said, leading them toward the far side of the lot. Mallory's eyes narrowed, scanning the area with a practiced gaze.

Josie stepped up beside Ryan, her voice low. "You think this one is connected to the other disappearances?" she asked.

Ryan didn't answer right away. He glanced over at Garret, who was watching the scene with the same intensity. "We'll find out soon enough," Garret replied.

Mallory stepped closer to the car, analyzing the open door and the empty seat where Natalie's belongings sat. Somewhere in the distance, the wind howled, which sent a shiver through Mallory's bones. She straightened, her hand instinctively brushing the gun at her side.

"Let's get to work," Garret said.

Mallory glanced at Ben. "You said the owner called it in?"

He nodded. "Yeah, he's in the lodge. I told him you'd probably want to speak with him."

Mallory shot Garret a glance. "Why don't you and I go check it out?"

Inside the lodge, Amos Jameson stood at the entrance, his posture radiating calculated confidence in a sharp suit that was impeccably pressed. He extended his hand to Mallory, his smile calculated—too smooth, too practiced. His eyes gleamed with the quiet confidence of a man who thought he had already sized them up.

"Amos Jameson," he said smoothly, his voice dripping with arrogance but dressed in the veneer of politeness. "I own Ridgeview Lodge. I'm the one who reported Natalie missing. She was my employee." He turned to Garret, offering the sheriff a practiced handshake. "Sheriff Cole, always a pleasure. Though I do wish it were under better circumstances."

"Thank you for speaking with us, Mr. Jameson," Mallory said.

Garrett crossed his arms and narrowed his eyes. "Mr. Jameson," he said with a polite nod, "do you have any idea why the security cameras were off?"

The smile on Amos's face faltered, a flicker of discomfort that was gone as quickly as it had appeared. "I asked my tech guy about that. Apparently, it was a maintenance issue. Very unfortunate timing, of course. But I can't imagine that it has anything to do with Natalie's disappearance."

Garret raised an eyebrow. "Yes, very unfortunate indeed," he said.

"We'll probably have you come down to the station to answer some more questions," Mallory responded, her voice laced with restrained professionalism. "So, don't leave the state." She gave him a tight nod, turning on her heel as she motioned for Garret to follow her.

Mallory and Garret made their way toward Natalie's locker, hoping to find something useful. The small space was cluttered with personal items and an old book on the history of Blackwater Ridge. Garret picked it up, flipping through the pages absently before a small, folded piece of paper fell from between the pages. He caught it before it hit the floor and handed it to Mallory.

Mallory unfolded the paper with care.

>Don't go near the ridge.
>It isn't safe. You've seen too much as it is.
>You need to leave town before you end up like the other girls.

Garret swore under his breath. "What the hell is this?"

"Well, this changes things," Mallory murmured. "If someone sent this to Natalie, she may have stumbled onto something."

Before they could continue, the soft click of shoes on the hardwood floor interrupted them. Amos appeared in the doorway, his hands tucked casually in his pockets, his dark eyes glinting as he looked between them. "Find anything?" he asked, his tone casual.

Garret quickly slipped the note into his jacket pocket, his expression neutral. "Just routine stuff," he replied smoothly, offering a forced smile. Amos nodded and walked away. As soon as he was out of earshot, Garret leaned in toward Mallory and whispered, "I think he saw us find that note."

Mallory glanced toward the hallway where Amos had disappeared. "Yeah. I'm sure he did. I've got a bad feeling about that guy, but if he's hiding something, he'll slip up."

Outside Ridgeview Lodge, Garrett stood by Boone and addressed the group of police officers standing on the lawn. "I'm Sheriff Garrett Cole, of Blackwater Ridge. As you know, we've had some missing women, so this is a joint effort between our departments. We also have FBI agent Mallory Crane assisting."

He nodded at Mallory, and she held her hand up.

"So, listen up," he continued. "We've got a missing woman, Natalie Baxter. I need everyone to spread out and search the area. We're looking for anything that could give us a lead. Personal belongings, signs of a struggle, or any clues that point us to where she might have gone."

Boone growled softly at Garret's side, and Mallory stepped forward. "We need to cover as much ground as possible. If you find anything that might connect Natalie to the other missing women, let us know. Don't assume anything—check every lead."

"Stay in touch," Garret added. "Don't go off alone. Keep each other in sight. And don't forget—this place can be dangerous. Be careful."

With that, the team spread out. Officers moved in pairs, their boots scraping the gravel as they headed toward the trees. Garret gave a quick nod to Mallory, and they began walking in the opposite direction, heading toward a trail that led deeper into the woods. Boone trotted beside them, his nose to the ground, sniffing intently.

As they walked through the trees, Mallory's hand rested lightly on the strap of her holster, her eyes darting from one side to the other, alert for any sign of movement.

Boone suddenly stopped, his ears erect and his nose twitching. "What is it, boy?" Garrett muttered.

The dog's gaze was fixed on something ahead. He trotted a few steps forward, then stopped again, sniffing at the ground.

"Stay close," Garret murmured to Mallory, his voice low.

Mallory nodded as she followed Garret's lead. Boone, still sniffing, tugged them toward a thick patch of trees. After a few more steps, Garret pushed through a thicket of branches and froze. There, partially obscured by the overgrowth, was the edge of something half hidden by the shadows of the trees.

"A shack," Garret whispered.

The building was small, rundown, and camouflaged by the dense foliage.

Mallory's gut twisted. "This isn't on any of the maps. I don't think it's part of the lodge."

Boone was still alert, his body stiff and his ears pricked. Garret motioned for Mallory to stay back as he approached the shack carefully. He didn't draw his weapon, but his hand hovered near it as he stepped through the underbrush.

The shack stood at the edge of the clearing, its windows boarded up. Garret crouched down to inspect the dirt beneath his feet, his eyes scanning the ground for anything that might stand out. Boone's growls became more frequent, his nose twitching with increasing intensity.

"Easy, boy," Garret whispered, trying to soothe the dog.

Mallory stood at a distance, her eyes darting to the shadows that crept along the edges of the clearing, her gun drawn. Suddenly, Boone broke away from Garret's side, darting toward the shack with a sudden burst of energy.

Garret cursed softly, pushing through the brush after him. "Boone," Garret called. "Come back!"

The dog was already at the door, sniffing around it furiously. Garret reached him just as Boone pawed at the dirt near the doorframe, uncovering a small object. Garret bent down, his fingers brushing over the soil to find a piece of torn fabric—dark, like the remnants of clothing.

"Shit," Garret muttered, standing up quickly. "This looks like it's from a uniform."

Mallory moved forward, her breath catching in her throat as she looked at the torn fabric. "You think it's Natalie's?" she asked.

"It's possible," Garret said grimly. He glanced at Boone, who had moved to the side, his nose still buried in the dirt. "But it could also be from one of the others."

As Mallory surveyed the shack, a cold sensation crawled up her spine. "We need to look inside."

The door creaked loudly as Garett pushed it open, the hinges groaning in protest. Inside, the air was stale and musty with the smell of rot. The floor was littered with old debris, broken furniture, and—something else.

"Something feels off," Mallory said, her voice tight.

Garret nodded, his eyes darting over the shadows in the corners.

Boone's growls returned, louder now, as he moved toward a corner of the shack where a small pile of old blankets lay. Garret and Mallory exchanged a glance before Garret stepped forward, his pulse quickening. When he reached the blankets, he lifted them carefully, and underneath, he found a small metal box—rusted but intact. It wasn't locked, and Garret opened it without hesitation.

Inside, there were several old photographs, some frayed and yellowed with age. One in particular caught his eye—a picture of a young woman with dark hair, standing in front of the church on Blackwater Ridge.

Mallory leaned over his shoulder to get a better look. "Is that... Susannah Fairchild?" she asked.

"I don't know. This just keeps getting weirder," Garret muttered, shoving the photographs back into the box. "But at least it's something."

THAT NIGHT, THE DIMLY lit conference room at the station buzzed with a mix of exhaustion and determination. Mallory, Garret, Ryan, and Josie sat around the long table, with folders and photos spread out in front of them. Boone lay at Garret's feet, his ears twitching occasionally as he dozed.

Garret raked his fingers through his hair and let out a frustrated sigh, leaning back in his chair. "Alright," he said, his voice carrying the edge of fatigue. "Let's go over the facts. We need to figure out where we go from here."

Mallory tapped her pen against the table. "Before we dive into what each of us found today, let's recap what we know so far about the four missing women."

Josie stood, moving to the victim board pinned with photos, notes, and maps. She pointed to the first photo, her voice steady. "Sadie Harper, thirty. Her boyfriend reported her missing four weeks ago after she didn't return from a solo hike near the ridge. He said she wanted to clear her head and take some photos of an area she'd discovered a few days earlier."

Ryan joined her, gesturing to the next photo. "Lila Dawson, twenty-two. She was reported missing three weeks ago by her father when she didn't show up for dinner as planned. A local, Peter Clark, saw her heading toward the ridge with a bag over her shoulder and her camera in hand."

Josie moved her finger to the next image, her brow furrowed. "Claire Crawford, twenty-five. Her car was found abandoned just last week. A passerby reported it after thinking it looked out of place. We have no idea why she was out near the lodge or where she went from there."

Garret added, "And Natalie Baxter, twenty-one. She was last seen this evening before her shift at Ridgeview Lodge. Amos Jameson, her boss, reported her missing after finding her car but no sign of her. We also found a note in her locker that seemed like a warning."

Mallory crossed her arms. "Four women. Four disappearances. All near the ridge. No witnesses. No solid leads. And nothing connecting them directly except the location."

The room fell silent for a moment before Garret leaned forward and pulled a folded piece of paper from his bag. "Oh yeah. We did find something today, though," he said, holding it out. "This letter. We discovered it in the cave where we found that scrap of Claire's jacket."

Mallory took the paper from him. "This is from Susannah. To Esther." Clearing her throat, Mallory read aloud. "'My Dearest Esther, the days pass with a most unrelenting heaviness, and with each, my condition grows yet more burdensome. The child that Tobias left me stirs within, a living proof of all that has been lost. I feel its life as surely as I feel the weight of my own despair.

"'It has been so long since they brought me to this wretched place that time itself has become a stranger to me. I know not how many days or weeks have passed, only that my thoughts are consumed with dread—for my babe, this innocent soul who has done no wrong. I tremble more for its fate than for mine own.

"'I cannot fathom why they keep me thus, nor for what cruel purpose I was chosen. I am alone, save for the silent figure who lingers ever at the mouth of this cavern. He is a shadow, ever watchful, yet never speaking. I am certain he fears that, should he give voice, I might know him. As for the Reverend—when he does deign to speak—his words are riddles and horrors. I have pleaded for mercy, for the life of my child, even should mine own be forfeit. Yet he only laughs, a sound colder than the grave, and whispers of a purpose yet to be fulfilled.

"'Oh, Esther, how my heart aches for Tobias—your dear brother, my beloved. How could I have foreseen that our love would lead to such an end? That I would be left to bear his child in this godforsaken place? I sought none of this. Had I never crossed paths with the Bennington family, never stepped foot within their cursed church, perhaps I should not now find myself ensnared in this fate most dire. I rue the choices that led me here with every breath that yet lingers in my breast.

"'In the silence of the night, strange voices rise from the very stone, whispers that chill me to the marrow. Shadows flicker and shift where none should be, and at times I glimpse figures in the darkness—spirits, perchance, of those long departed. At first, I deemed it mere fancy, the wanderings of a mind frayed by despair, but now I know not what to believe. They bear the countenance of Cherokee phantoms, and though they speak not, their presence fills me with a dread I scarce can name.

"'I pray for thy safety, Esther, and that thou mayest yet find some means of escaping the shadow that now looms over this place. I know not if this letter shall ever find thee, but in the writing of it, I take what small solace I may. It is as though, in these words, I reach across the abyss to thee, my dearest and truest friend.

"'Pray for me, Esther. Pray for my child, the life yet quickening within me. And know that I love thee, now and evermore. Mayest thou yet find joy where I could not Thine always, Susannah.'"

As Mallory finished reading, silence hung thick in the room.

Josie swallowed hard and whispered, "She... she was pregnant. And they kept her there, like an animal."

"Hold on," Mallory said with impatience. "We don't even know if Susannah actually wrote this. It could be a forgery. We need to authenticate it—I'll send it off for analysis and have it date-stamped."

Garret dragged a hand down his face. "Yeah, but if it *is* real, it sounds like Susannah knew too much."

Mallory exhaled sharply and set the letter down, her jaw tight. "Let's say it is real. All it proves is that Silas Bennington had something to do with Susannah's disappearance—a case that's over a century old. And frankly, I'm getting tired of this twisted history lesson. We have four missing women right now—possibly dead. The only way this 'story' matters is if someone out there is trying to finish what Silas Bennington started."

Ryan nodded. "I'm telling you. It's a cult, and it's all connected. I feel it in my bones."

Mallory exhaled sharply. "I don't disagree," she said, her voice softer now. "But we can't solve this case on gut feelings. We need proof—something solid. And we need it now, before another woman disappears."

Chapter Ten

The next morning, Mallory pushed open the heavy wooden door of the sheriff's office and made her way to the conference room where Garret was staring at a large map spread out across the table, dotted with markers and notes from their investigation. Mallory leaned over it, tracing her finger along the winding trails that connected the cave, the old church, and the lodge.

"All of this seems to center around the ridge and that church," she said. "If we're going to stop whatever's going on, we need to figure out where the women are. I think they were at the cave, but where did they take them after that?"

Garret hesitated, then cleared his throat. "There's an old hunting cabin near the summit of the ridge," he admitted. "It's been closed up for years—at least, it's supposed to be. It's secluded, nothing else around for miles except that old church. If someone wanted to keep people hidden, it'd be the perfect spot."

Mallory's eyes narrowed. "And you're just now telling me this?"

Garret sighed, rubbing a hand over his face before leaning against the table. "It's my cabin," he said. "Been in my family for generations. My dad... he was obsessed with the ridge, always talking about its power like it was something mystical. I thought it was just his way of coping after we lost my mom. But now, with everything happening, I'm wondering if there was more to it."

Mallory studied him, her expression unreadable. She knew Garret—had known him since they were kids—but this? This was sloppy. "So, you haven't been out there since the first woman went missing?"

"No," he admitted. "Honestly, I didn't even think about it until we looked at the cave."

Mallory exhaled sharply. "We need to check it out. *Now*. If there's even the slightest chance any of the women are there, we can't waste time."

Garret looked away, his jaw tight. "I know," he said quietly. "I haven't been back since my dad died ten years ago. But you're right. Let's go."

The truck's tires crunched over the winding, narrow road climbing the ridge, the cabin hidden deep within the forest—the kind of place no one would stumble across unless they knew exactly where to look. The tension in the cab was thick, suffocating. Mallory sat rigid beside him, one hand resting on her holstered weapon, her gaze locked on the shifting shadows beyond the windshield.

The cabin finally came into view, a weathered structure half-swallowed by vines and overgrowth. Its shutters hung crooked, and the roof sagged slightly, but it was still intact. Garret killed the engine, and the silence that followed was deafening.

"Stay alert," Mallory said, stepping out of the truck and motioning for Boone to follow. The dog bounded down, his nose to the ground as he sniffed the air.

Garret unholstered his weapon and followed Mallory up the creaking steps to the cabin door. It was partially ajar, with a faint trail of dirt leading inside. They exchanged a glance before Garret nodded, pushing the door open with the barrel of his gun.

Inside, the air was stale and heavy, carrying the scent of damp wood and something faintly metallic. The single-room cabin was sparsely furnished, with a cot in one corner, an old table, and a stone fireplace. Boone let out a low whine and darted to the back of the cabin, his nose pressed to the floorboards near the cot.

Mallory followed him, and her breath caught when she saw the figure curled up on the thin mattress. "Sadie Harper," she whispered.

The woman was filthy, her hair matted with dirt, her clothes torn and stained. Her skin was pale, her lips dry and cracked, and her eyes stared ahead, unfocused. She flinched as Mallory knelt beside her.

"Sadie," Mallory said softly, her tone gentle but urgent. "My name's Mallory Crane. I'm an FBI agent, and I'm here to help you. You're safe now."

Sadie didn't respond. Her chest rose and fell in shallow breaths, her body trembling.

Mallory reached for her canteen and uncapped it. "Here," she coaxed, pressing it lightly to Sadie's lips. "Just a sip."

The water seemed to stir something in Sadie. Her lips parted, and she took a hesitant sip before coughing weakly. Her eyes darted around the room, wild and unfocused, before settling on Mallory. She tried to speak, but the words came out in a dry rasp.

"You're okay now," Mallory assured her, glancing back at Garret. "We need to get her to the hospital."

Garret nodded, holstering his weapon and pulling his radio from his belt. "This is Sheriff Cole," he said. "We've found Sadie Harper at the old hunting cabin off Elk Road near the ridge. She's alive but in rough shape. Requesting immediate medical assistance."

Mallory turned back to Sadie, her hand gently brushing a strand of hair from the woman's face. "Sadie, can you tell us anything? What happened to you? Who brought you here?"

Sadie's lips moved, but no sound came. Her eyes filled with tears, and she shook her head, her body trembling harder.

Mallory squeezed her hand gently. "It's okay," she said softly. "You don't have to talk right now. We've got you."

Garret crouched beside them, his face etched with worry. "Whoever did this could still be out there," he murmured. "We need to move fast."

THE SHARP SCENT OF antiseptic hung heavy in the hospital room. Sadie Harper looked frail under the harsh fluorescent lights, her sunken eyes darting nervously between Garrett and Mallory. Her face was pale and gaunt, framed by hair that looked dull and unkempt, but there was a flicker of determination in her gaze—a small ember of survival.

Mallory pulled up a chair to the bed. "Sadie, we know this is overwhelming, but we need your help. Anything you can tell us, anything at all, could save lives."

Sadie swallowed hard and nodded. Her voice trembled as she spoke. "I... I'll try. I want to help. I just don't know how much I remember. It's all... it's like a nightmare I can't wake up from."

Garret leaned against the wall, his face a mask of quiet resolve. "Start wherever you feel comfortable," he said, his deep voice reassuring. "You're safe now, Sadie."

She hesitated, her fingers fidgeting with the blanket. "They... they took me when I was hiking. I didn't even see them coming. One minute, I was taking pictures near the ridge, and the next, I felt something hit me from behind.

When I woke up, I was in a dark chamber. It might have been a cave, but I'm not really sure because I couldn't see anything."

Mallory exchanged a glance with Garret before pressing gently, "Do you know who took you? Did you see their faces?"

Sadie shook her head, her shoulders trembling. "No. They always wore masks. Long robes, too, like something out of an old horror movie. They never let us see who they were. I tried to listen to their voices, to figure out if I recognized them, but they were careful. Always whispered, always distorted."

Mallory leaned forward, her tone encouraging. "You said 'us.' Did you see the other missing women? Lila, Claire, Natalie—were they there with you?"

Sadie nodded slowly, her eyes welling up with tears. "I saw them, but we weren't allowed to talk. They kept us separate most of the time. I only caught glimpses—Lila crying when they dragged her out of one of the rooms, Claire looking so pale and scared. And Natalie... I didn't see her much, but I think she was new. She looked like she was still trying to understand what was happening."

"What rooms?" Mallory asked, her brow furrowing as she turned her curious gaze toward Garret before shifting her attention back to Sadie.

Sadie hesitated, her fingers twisting the edge of the blanket that covered her lap. Her voice wavered, barely above a whisper. "I don't know for sure," she admitted, her eyes darting nervously around the room as though she expected the shadows to spring to life. "They moved us a lot. It was hard to keep track of where we were."

Mallory leaned in slightly, her tone softening. "Take your time, Sadie. Anything you can remember could help."

Sadie swallowed hard, the words seeming to catch in her throat before tumbling out. "One time... I think it was a basement. The air was damp and cold, and it smelled like dirt and mildew. There were these small rooms, like cubicles or cells, all separated. They didn't have doors, though. Just open spaces."

Her hands trembled as she gestured, trying to convey what she had seen.

"Sometimes, I could see into the other rooms. Not clearly, but enough to catch glimpses. I saw shadows moving. I think... I think it was the others."

Garret straightened, his expression darkening. "No doors?" he asked. "Like they wanted you to see each other?"

Sadie nodded hesitantly. "Maybe. I don't know. It was like they didn't care if we saw... or maybe they wanted us to feel trapped, hopeless. Like there was no escape."

Mallory exchanged a grim look with Garret before turning back to Sadie. "You're doing great, Sadie. Do you remember anything else about the basement? Anything at all—the sounds, the people, anything unusual?"

Sadie stared at the blanket for a moment, her brows knitting together as she searched her fragmented memories. "I remember hearing voices," she murmured. "Low, muffled. Like they didn't want us to know what they were saying. And footsteps... always footsteps echoing down the hall. It felt like they were everywhere, always watching."

Garret's jaw tightened, his mind racing with the implications. "What did they want with you? Did they ever say why they were keeping you there?"

Sadie's hands clenched the blanket, her knuckles white. "They kept talking about the darkness. About feeding it. They said we were part of the greater good... that our pain, our lives, were necessary to bring it forward." Her voice broke, and she covered her face with trembling hands. "It didn't make any sense, but they believed it. They believed it so much."

Mallory reached out, placing a comforting hand on Sadie's arm. "Take your time," she said softly. "What do you mean by the darkness? Did they ever explain it?"

Sadie lowered her hands, her eyes wide with fear. "No, not really. They just said it was ancient, older than anything we could imagine. That it needed us to wake up, to grow stronger. They... uh... they called it a ritual. A sacrifice for the greater good."

Mallory felt a chill run down her spine but kept her expression neutral. "Did they ever mention names? A leader? Someone who was in charge?"

Sadie hesitated, her brow furrowing. "There was one name... I kept hearing it. Silas. Silas Bennington. They spoke about him like he was some kind of prophet." She paused, her voice dropping to a whisper. "I think I saw him."

Mallory blinked, caught off guard. "You saw him?"

Sadie nodded fervently. "Yes. He came to the cave once. He was tall, with these piercing eyes that seemed to see right through you. He wore old-fashioned clothes, like something from another century, and he just stood there, watching us."

Garret frowned, exchanging a skeptical glance with Mallory. "Sadie, Silas Bennington was a reverend in the late 1800s. He's been dead for over a century."

Sadie shook her head vehemently. "I know what I saw. I'm not crazy. It was him. I heard the others whispering about him, too. They said he was the one who started all of this, that he's been guiding them all along."

"Could it have been someone pretending to be him? Someone using his name to scare you?" Mallory asked.

"I don't know," Sadie admitted. "But it felt real. Too real. And those whispers... those shadows... it was like the darkness they talked about was alive. I could feel it watching me."

"Sadie, you've been through something unimaginable. We're going to do everything we can to figure this out and stop whoever's behind it. But you need to focus on resting and recovering for now," Mallory said.

Sadie nodded weakly, her eyes brimming with tears. "I just want to go home. I just want this to be over."

Garret stepped closer, his voice firm but kind. "You're safe now, Sadie. And we're not going to stop until we get to the bottom of this. I promise."

In the hallway, Mallory turned to Garrett. "I guess that proves our cult theory."

"You think she's hallucinating about Silas?" he asked.

Mallory hesitated before replying. "I don't know whether she was hallucinating or if someone dressed like him, but it shows that somebody still believes in the crazy shit Silas Bennington started hundreds of years ago."

Garret nodded, his jaw set. "Yeah. We need to move fast on this. Whoever's behind this stuff isn't going to stop. And if Sadie's right about the ritual..."

He didn't finish the thought, but the unspoken fear hung heavy between them.

"I'm going to put a call in to my boss. I want at least one more agent down here to help us with this. We need to make sure someone is standing guard over Sadie at all times. Someone I know we can trust." Mallory said as she glanced back toward Sadie's room.

THE CHAMBER WAS DIM and oppressive, lit only by the flickering glow of a single lantern swaying gently from a rusty hook embedded in the damp stone ceiling. Shadows leaped and danced across the walls, elongating the jagged edges of the ancient stones until they seemed like claws reaching out from the darkness. The air was thick with the scent of damp earth and mildew, and it clung to the skin like an unwelcome shroud.

A figure paced the uneven floor, the sharp strike of boots punctuating the tense silence. Each step was measured and deliberate yet betrayed an underlying fury. Their cloak swirled with each turn, brushing the ground as they pivoted sharply.

"They found Sadie Harper," the figure growled, the words escaping through clenched teeth. Their voice was a low snarl, taut with barely restrained anger. "She was supposed to stay hidden, out of their reach. Now they've ruined everything. Months—years of work—undone because of their meddling."

Leaning lazily against a wooden support beam, another figure observed the outburst with an air of detached amusement. Their posture was relaxed, one leg crossed over the other, arms folded across their chest, but their eyes—sharp and gleaming like shards of glass—betrayed a cunning intelligence. A faint smirk played on their lips as they responded, their voice smooth and deliberate.

"Calm yourself," they said, the words slicing through the tension with a practiced ease. "This isn't the disaster you think it is. In fact, I'd argue it's an opportunity."

The pacing stopped abruptly, and the first figure turned sharply, their face twisted in a mask of frustration and disbelief. Their fists curled tightly at their sides, their knuckles white. "Not a disaster? She was vital to the plan! We *needed* her. The Darkness needed her. And now—now she's in their hands!"

A cold chuckle echoed through the chamber, carrying an edge that seemed to reverberate in the stone walls. The second figure pushed off the beam and stepped forward, the shadows playing tricks with their features, making them seem almost otherworldly.

"Needed her?" they repeated, their tone mocking and dripping with confidence. "You're thinking too small. She was a tool, nothing more—a means to an end. But tools can be replaced. And now, we have something better."

Confusion flickered behind the first figure's fury, their expression tightening as they demanded, "Better? What could possibly be better? She was part of the bloodline! She was the key."

The second figure's smirk widened, their eyes gleaming with a dark satisfaction. They stepped closer, their voice low and conspiratorial, yet filled with undeniable certainty. "Think," they said, the word drawn out as if speaking to a child. "She was useful because of the bloodline, yes. But she wasn't the only one, was she? There's another."

Realization dawned slowly, creeping across the first figure's face like an unwelcome chill. Their fury gave way to a simmering dread as the pieces began to fall into place. "You're talking about *her*," they said, their voice almost a whisper, tinged with disbelief.

"Of course," the second figure said, their tone smug and triumphant. "She's connected—more deeply than the others. And unlike the ones we had to *find*, she's walking straight into our trap, step by step. All we have to do is wait."

The first figure's shoulders tensed, and they took a step closer, their fists trembling with the effort to maintain control. "And if you're wrong?" they spat, their voice low and dangerous. "If she doesn't take the bait, if she figures it out—what then? Do you realize what's at stake? If we fail—if she escapes—it's over. Everything. Gone."

The second figure's confidence was unshaken. They shrugged, brushing the concern aside like an inconsequential nuisance. "I'm not wrong," they said firmly, their voice steady as stone. "She won't walk away. She's too determined, too curious for her own good. Her bloodline is tied to this place, to *us*. It's inescapable. She'll lead herself right to where we need her. And when the time comes, she'll serve the purpose far better than the one they found."

For a moment, silence enveloped the chamber, broken only by the faint, rhythmic drip of water somewhere in the distance. The first figure turned away, their hands gripping the edge of a crude wooden table, shoulders heaving with the weight of their thoughts. When they finally spoke, their voice was tight, edged with reluctant agreement.

"If you're wrong, we lose everything. The Darkness cannot be denied—if it is, it will turn on *us*." They turned back, their eyes locking with the second figure's, searching for any sign of doubt but finding none. "I hope your arrogance doesn't doom us all."

"I'm not wrong," the second figure repeated, their unwavering certainty infuriating and yet somehow infectious. "Let them have their small victory with her. It changes nothing. Soon enough, she'll be ours. Everything is in motion."

The lantern flickered, the light momentarily dimming before steadying again. Shadows stretched and twisted, clawing at the walls as the two figures stared at each other, their expressions mirrored in their dark intent.

The second figure let out a low chuckle, the sound chilling in the otherwise silent chamber. "You'll see," they said, their voice soft but dripping with confidence. "Soon, all their efforts will crumble. Let them think they've won for now. It won't matter. The bloodline will serve as it always has—whether they want it to or not."

Chapter Eleven

Mallory pulled her phone from her pocket as she climbed out of Garret's truck. The gravel crunched under her boots as she made her way toward the side entrance of the Ridgeview Sheriff's Department. Her fingers hesitated over the screen before she hit the call button for Richard Larkin, her boss at the Bureau.

The phone rang twice before his familiar voice answered, warm and full of its usual energy. "Crane! How's things going in Tennessee? Found those missing hikers yet, or are you just enjoying the mountain air?"

Mallory let out a quiet sigh and leaned against the wall of the building, the cool stone grounding her. "Not quite, sir," she said, her voice carrying a serious tone that immediately caused Larkin to pause.

"What's going on?" he asked, his tone sobering.

"We were able to find one of the missing women," Mallory began, keeping her voice calm and measured. "Sadie Harper. But there are still three others unaccounted for, and one of them—Natalie Baxter—was taken less than twenty-four hours ago."

"Damn," Larkin muttered, the gravity of the situation sinking in. "Have you been able to connect the dots yet? Do we have any suspects?"

Mallory took a steadying breath. "That's the thing, sir. I think we're dealing with something much bigger than just a kidnapping ring. This isn't random, and it's not new. It ties back to cases that go back decades—maybe over a century."

There was silence on the other end of the line. She imagined Larkin leaning back in his chair, rubbing his temples as he processed her words.

"Crane," he said slowly, "are you telling me you're chasing some kind of historical conspiracy? You know how that sounds, right?"

"I do, sir," she admitted, her tone firm but respectful. "And I wouldn't be saying it if I didn't have reason to believe it was true. There's a church on the ridge—a small, abandoned place. We think it's connected to the disappearances, both the recent ones and the ones from the past. Sadie mentioned it, and we've found evidence that leads back to it. But that's not the worst of it."

Larkin let out a low exhale. "Alright, Crane, hit me. What's the worst of it?"

"The mayor," Mallory said, her voice sharpening. "Mayor Darla Hensley. I think she's tied to this. Her family has been involved in that church for generations. And she's doing everything in her power to stall the investigation. She's blocked warrants, denied access to resources, and leaned hard on the Sheriff's Department to keep things quiet."

"You're accusing a sitting mayor of obstructing an active FBI investigation?" Larkin asked, his voice a mix of disbelief and caution.

"Yes, sir," Mallory replied without hesitation. "I don't have hard evidence yet, but her interference isn't subtle. Every time we get close to something, she's there to derail it. It's not a coincidence."

Larkin was silent for a long moment, and Mallory could hear the faint tapping of his fingers on his desk. "You're walking a fine line here, Crane," he said finally. "If you go after a mayor without solid proof, it could blow up in your face. You know that, right?"

"I know," she said, her tone clipped. "That's why I'm being careful. But I need your help, sir. We found Sadie Harper in an old hunting cabin, miles from the nearest road. Whoever took her didn't plan on her being found. They'll come after her if they think she knows something. I need agents I can trust to keep her safe."

"You don't trust the local deputies?" Larkin asked, though his tone suggested he already knew the answer.

"It's not that, sir," Mallory said firmly. "The Sheriff's Department is understaffed and under pressure. Besides, Hensley's influence runs deep, and I don't trust deputizing new officers in this town. I can't risk Sadie's safety on the off chance that someone is compromised. I need someone I can count on."

Larkin let out a soft hum of consideration. "You're asking me to pull agents from other cases and send them into a small-town mess that could be political as much as criminal. That's a big ask, Crane."

"I wouldn't ask if it weren't necessary," Mallory replied, her voice steady. "This isn't just about protecting Sadie. It's about stopping whoever's behind this before they take someone else. The longer we wait, the more danger these women are in."

Larkin sighed heavily, the sound crackling through the phone. "Alright, Crane. I'll send Archer and Morgan. They're some of my best. Archer has worked some cult cases, which may be helpful if you're talking about a church and something that goes back a century. Morgan's had experience with witness protection. Plus, they're both only about an hour or two away from your current location. But I'm warning you—this had better be as serious as you're making it out to be. I don't want to be answering questions about why I diverted resources for a wild goose chase."

"It's serious," Mallory said, her voice resolute. "Thank you, sir."

"Before you go," Larkin added, his tone sharp. "What actually do you know about the church? You said the missing woman mentioned it."

Mallory hesitated, choosing her words carefully. "Long story short, sir, Sadie mentioned a name—Silas Bennington. He was a reverend connected to the church back in the late 1800s. According to her, she saw him while she was being held."

"Crane," Larkin said slowly, "are you seriously telling me a kidnapping victim saw a man who's been dead for over a century?"

"She's been through a lot," Mallory said, deflecting slightly. "Dehydration, trauma—it's possible she was hallucinating. Or it's possible someone's using his name to intimidate her. I don't know yet. But whatever's going on, the name keeps coming up. It's something we can't ignore."

Larkin let out a low grunt, his skepticism clear. "You're in deep with this one, Crane. Alright, I'll give you the support you need, but you'd better be ready to explain all of this when it's over. And if you find concrete evidence of Hensley's involvement, I want it on my desk immediately. Understood?"

"Understood," Mallory said, a note of gratitude in her voice.

"Good. Keep me updated, and don't do anything reckless," Larkin said, his tone softening slightly.

Mallory's lips twitched in a faint smile. "I'll be careful, sir. Thank you."

"Stay vigilant, Crane," Larkin said before the line disconnected.

Mallory lowered the phone and slipped it back into her pocket. The conversation had gone better than she'd expected, but the weight of the investigation still pressed heavily on her shoulders. Taking a deep breath, she straightened and headed into the station.

Mallory stepped into Garret's office, the creaking of the wooden floorboards breaking the stillness as she entered. Garret was sitting behind his cluttered desk, his attention momentarily fixed on a stack of paperwork, but his eyes lifted when she walked in. The tired lines on his face softened slightly, though the constant tension never fully left his expression.

"How'd the conversation with your boss go?" Garret asked, his voice low but laced with genuine curiosity.

Mallory let out a tight, controlled breath, her fingers absentmindedly playing with the hem of her sleeve. She nodded, her jaw set in a firm line. "It went better than I thought it would. I think it helps that I don't ask for things very often," she replied.

Tossing his pen onto the desk, Garret leaned back in his chair with a soft groan. The creak of the old leather chair echoed in the quiet room as he looked at Mallory, his gaze serious yet understanding. "So, is he sending someone to help us guard Sadie?" he asked.

She gave a small nod. "Yeah, he's sending Logan Archer and Elizabeth Morgan. They're both some of the best on our team. Archer's an expert on cults, and Morgan's got experience with protection detail. Logan's a former Marine, and Lizzie's former Navy."

Garret raised an eyebrow, his mouth curling into a half-smile. "Impressive. Sounds like they'll be great to have as backup."

She shrugged and let out a tired sigh. "The best part?" she asked, pausing for a moment as she locked eyes with him. "I know both of them won't mock me when it comes to the supernatural crap we're dealing with. They both grew up in the Appalachian Mountains and have told me some pretty creepy stories."

Garret chuckled, a soft sound that didn't quite reach the exhaustion in his eyes. "Guess we have that in common with them then, huh?" he replied, a faint smile tugging at the corners of his lips.

"Yep."

"You starting to believe some of the supernatural stuff?" Garrett asked.

"Not a chance," Mallory replied curtly. "But I *do believe* that the people behind this shit believe it, and that's what matters."

Before Garrett could respond, a knock echoed from the door, followed by the sound of it creaking open. "Hey, guys," Ryan's voice came through, smooth but with a hint of urgency. "Josie and I might have something."

Mallory and Garret exchanged a glance before both of them pushed to their feet and followed Ryan out of the office and into the nearby conference room. They were met by Josie, who was already standing next to the table with a file laid out before her.

Ryan took a step forward and opened the file with a careful motion. "We've been looking into a few of the families that have been in the area since the town was founded," he said, his voice smooth with determination. "I think I have a lead." He glanced at Josie, who nodded in agreement.

Josie laid a fresh set of documents on the table, the sound of paper rustling filling the otherwise quiet room. "There are only a few founding families left in Blackwater Ridge, the Maynards being one of them," she said, her eyes glinting with the excitement of a breakthrough. "Records show that back in the 1890s, Elton Maynard was closely tied to Reverend Bennington and his congregation. In 1894, Silas Bennington deeded a large parcel of land to the Maynard family. And get this—part of that parcel includes part of the ridge that's only yards away from the church."

Mallory leaned forward, her brow furrowing in thought as she processed the information. "Maynard?" she asked, her voice sharp with curiosity. "Why does that name sound so familiar?"

Ryan nodded, picking up on her interest. "The Maynards were one of the oldest and most prominent families in the area. They've been around for generations, but they've kept a low profile recently. There's always been whispers about their connections to the church and the old congregation. Not much of it is confirmed, but the land Bennington gave them?" He leaned closer to the table, looking directly at Mallory. "We think this might be the key. The land is too close to the church to be a coincidence. And if the Maynards were involved with Bennington..."

Mallory rubbed her temples. "Jesus," she murmured. "If Bennington really gave the Maynards that land, it means they have a direct connection to whatever's been happening in that church. And if they're involved in these disappearances..." Her voice trailed off as her thoughts raced.

Josie, who had been watching Mallory carefully, spoke up. "We've tried to dig into the Maynards' current activities, but they're incredibly tight-lipped. They've managed to stay out of the public eye for years. However, one thing is clear—they're tied to the church in a way that no one else in this town is. I don't know if they're directly involved, but I wouldn't rule it out."

Garret, who had been quietly listening, finally spoke, his voice thoughtful. "The Maynards have always kept to themselves. If there's something going on with them, it's probably going to be harder to crack than we think. But if what Ryan and Josie are saying is true, this could be our link to everything."

Mallory nodded slowly. "We need to find out more about the Maynards—what their connection is to the church, to Bennington, and to whatever this darkness is. But right now, our priority has to be Sadie. We can't let anything happen to her."

Ryan nodded, his jaw tightening. "We've got her covered for now. But we should move quickly. If the Maynards are connected to this, they won't let us keep digging for long."

Mallory straightened, the edge of determination in her voice as she met each of their eyes. "We keep pushing forward. We need to be smart, but we can't wait. We'll find out what's going on in that church, and we'll get to the bottom of all this."

Garret's gaze locked onto Mallory's, his expression a mix of agreement and worry. "You're right. We can't let up."

THAT AFTERNOON, GARRET and Mallory arrived at Maggie Whitaker's house just as the sun was beginning to dip below the horizon. The late autumn air was crisp, carrying with it the scent of earth and pine, and the light fading over the mountains seemed to add a somber quality to the evening. Maggie was sitting on her porch swing, with a book in her hands. As soon as she saw them, she set the book down with a soft sigh and waved them over.

"Come on up, you two," she called, her voice warm but tinged with something else. "Let me make sure you're comfortable."

In her mid-eighties now, Maggie's auburn hair, now flecked with silver, framed her face in soft curls. The swing creaked as she gently rocked back and forth, waiting for Garret and Mallory to join her.

"Thank you for taking the time to talk to us again, Maggie," Mallory said as she took a seat on the swing beside her, trying to ease into the conversation. "We've been looking into the Maynard family, and we thought you might be able to help us understand more about them. You've lived here long enough to know how things have changed."

"Oh, dear, I don't know how much help I'll be," Maggie replied with a half-laugh. "But I'll do what I can." She adjusted her glasses and gave them both a look that seemed to weigh the question carefully. "The Maynards, huh? Well, you know, they've been a part of Blackwater Ridge for as long as anyone can remember. The family's history here goes back generations. But what exactly are you wanting to know?"

Garret glanced at Mallory and nodded for her to take the lead. Mallory cleared her throat. "We've been learning about the history of the church on the ridge and the Reverend, Silas Bennington. There are rumors about the Maynards being involved with him. We were hoping you might have some insight into that connection."

Maggie's eyes seemed to cloud over for a moment. She was quiet as she considered her words, her fingers fiddling with the edge of her book before she set it aside completely. When she finally spoke, her voice was slow, as if carefully untangling years of memory.

"The Maynards..." Maggie murmured, her gaze drifting far off into the distance. "Well, where to start with them? The family's always had its share of secrets. Some of them are more shadow than substance, and others... well, they're just too much to untangle." She paused, her lips pursed tightly as she gathered her thoughts. "But you're right to be curious about them, especially about Silas Bennington. When he came to town, the Maynards weren't far behind. They were part of what was happening, whether they liked it or not."

Garret leaned forward, his curiosity piqued. "How so? What kind of involvement did they have with Reverend Bennington?"

Maggie shifted in her seat, her hands folding in her lap as she began to speak again. "The Maynards have always been deeply tied to the land here. It's not just about owning property or making money. No, it's deeper than that.

They've been here since the town's founding, and there's something about that land—it's almost like it's... alive. And when Bennington came, well, it seems that whatever he was doing, whatever rituals he had planned, the Maynards were there to support him."

"Rituals?" Garret asked, his brow furrowed.

Maggie nodded slowly, her voice taking on a tone that seemed as old and weathered as the land itself. "If you've been digging, then I know you've heard about them. There were sacrifices and strange ceremonies. Those stories have been whispered about for as long as I've lived here, and maybe even longer. Some say Bennington was trying to open a door, a gateway to something ancient, something far older than any of us could understand. The Maynards—well, they were involved in those ceremonies. No one knows exactly how much they believed in it, but they were there. They were the ones who helped maintain the church, helped him with the land... and it wasn't just for show."

Mallory felt her stomach twist at the implications. "Maggie, if you knew about these ceremonies and stuff, why didn't you tell us about them the first time we came to see you?"

Maggie chuckled. "I know what people say about me—that I'm a crazy old lady. And if I would've told you about that from the beginning, you would've thought it, too. I knew you had to discover some of this on your own."

Mallory nodded. "Okay. But what about after Bennington left? What happened then?"

Maggie's face grew somber. She clasped her hands tighter, as if bracing herself. "That's where it gets tricky. The Bennington family left, sure, but the Maynards didn't just walk away from the church and its practices. They kept up the connection to the land. The rumors say they continued to practice in secret, carrying on whatever Bennington had started, but in the shadows. Some people said they were trying to protect the town, to keep something bad from happening. Others..." Maggie's voice trailed off as she seemed to consider her words carefully, "... well, others think they just wanted to keep the power for themselves."

Garret was silent for a moment, processing everything Maggie had just said. "What about Caleb Maynard? What can you tell me about him? He's the one who inherited the property recently."

Maggie's expression hardened slightly at the mention of his name. "Caleb Maynard... now, he's a different case altogether. He's young, but he's clever. He inherited the land from his grandfather just a few years ago, and since then, he's been trying to modernize things and bring in more development. The old Maynard place was falling apart, but Caleb's been pouring money into it, trying to make it something... different. I've heard rumors about what he's been doing out there, but honestly, I don't know the full story. He's always kept to himself, and people around here? They tend to stay away from the Maynard land. They always have."

Garret looked up, meeting Mallory's eyes for a brief moment before turning back to Maggie. "Have you heard anything... strange coming from the Maynard place?"

Maggie looked uncomfortable. She shifted her weight on the swing, avoiding eye contact for a second. "Sure. I've heard whispers, and I've seen things like lights in the windows late at night, figures moving around when no one's supposed to be there. People say they've seen strange gatherings at odd hours. But like I said, no one really dares to go up there and check. People around here... we've learned to leave certain things alone. And Caleb's been very careful about keeping to himself, making sure no one gets too close."

"Do you think Caleb knows what's going on?" Mallory asked.

Maggie paused, her eyes narrowing slightly. "I don't know. I want to think he doesn't, that he's not part of it all. But then again, if he doesn't know, why would he stay so close to all that power? Why hasn't he sold the land and moved on like others have? No, Caleb Maynard's tied up in this somehow. But whether it's by choice or not, I can't say."

"Thank you, Maggie," Garret said quietly, standing up from the swing. He tipped his hat to her and gave her a warm smile. "We appreciate everything you've shared with us."

Maggie's eyes softened, but there was still that hint of wariness in her gaze. "You two be careful, now. The Maynards... well, they may be part of this town's history, but that doesn't mean they're good for it. Some things are better left alone, especially when it comes to them."

Chapter Twelve

The small office felt stifling as Garret sat at his desk, flipping through a folder filled with case notes. The door swung open with a creak, and the familiar click of heels on the old wooden floor signaled the arrival of someone none too happy.

Darla Hensley, the mayor of Blackwater Ridge, stood in the doorway, her frame silhouetted by the soft light streaming through the cracked blinds. Her sharp eyes scanned the room, assessing everything with the kind of authority that had made her both respected and feared in this town. She strode inside, closing the door with a controlled motion that made it clear she wasn't here for a friendly chat.

"Garret," she said, her voice smooth but carrying an unmistakable edge. "We need to talk."

Garret didn't look up right away, though he could feel the tension in the air. His fingers drummed absently on the edge of the desk as he closed the folder, finally meeting her gaze. "What can I do for you, Mayor?"

"I heard you called in more FBI agents," Darla said, her eyes narrowing as she moved toward his desk, standing on the opposite side. "Is that really necessary? This is a small town, Garret. You don't need to escalate things like that."

Garret raised an eyebrow, leaning back in his chair. "I think it is. We've got missing women, and I'm not going to let this case slip through the cracks just because we're a small town. The FBI has the resources we need right now."

Darla's eyes flickered with frustration. She crossed her arms, the stern line of her lips betraying the irritation bubbling beneath the surface. "I don't care about the FBI, Garret. I care about this town. The people here are looking to you for answers, and you're inviting outsiders to come in and stir things up."

He pressed his lips together, his mind working quickly. "I'm not doing this for the FBI's benefit, Mayor. I'm doing it for the people of Blackwater Ridge.

If we don't get a handle on this now, it'll spread. We've already lost too much time."

Darla didn't respond right away. Instead, she took a step closer, her heels tapping on the floor with an almost rhythmic determination. "You're poking around where you shouldn't be, Garret," she said, her voice low now, more dangerous. "Why are you looking into the Maynard family? What's the connection there? You didn't think I'd notice that, did you?"

The words hit him like a punch to the gut. Garret's mind froze for a split second, the question hanging in the air like an invisible weight. His thoughts raced, his heartbeat quickening. They hadn't shared his findings with anyone yet—not about the Maynards, not the about church, and not about Reverend Bennington's ties to the whole situation. The only ones who knew were people in his department, Mallory, her boss, and Maggie.

Darla took another step forward, her presence looming over him now. "I asked you a question, Garret. Why the Maynards? You're not just chasing ghosts, are you?" Her voice was sharp, cutting through the room like a knife.

Garret clenched the armrest of his chair, the metal digging into his palm as he forced himself to maintain control. He tilted his head slightly, trying to gauge her reaction. "The Maynards have been tied to the church for over a century. They're a central part of this town's history, and now we've found a connection between them and the missing women. It's a lead, Mayor. That's all. I'm not just going to ignore it."

Darla's lips curled into a smile, but it was cold—calculating. "Is that so? Funny, I didn't think the Maynards would be part of your investigation. They've always kept a low profile. But you—" she gestured to him with a flick of her fingers, "You've been digging into their family's past. It's almost like you're trying to stir something up, Garret. I'm not sure what you're after, but I can't let you go down that path. There's too much at stake."

"Too much at stake?" Garret asked, his voice laced with suspicion. "What exactly do you mean by that, Mayor? Because from where I'm standing, it looks like you're more concerned about protecting certain families than solving this case."

Darla's smile didn't falter. In fact, it seemed to widen just slightly, but there was no warmth behind it. "You misunderstand, Garret. I'm concerned about the people of this town. About keeping things in order. The Maynards are old money. They've been here since the beginning. You start pulling on their thread, and you might unravel the whole town."

Garret sat up straighter in his chair, his fingers pressing into the wood of the desk. "I'm not backing down, Darla. If the Maynards are involved in something dark, I'm going to find out what it is. And I'm not letting anyone stop me."

"Don't make this harder than it has to be, Garret," Darla said, her voice now taking on a warning tone. "You don't want to find yourself on the wrong side of this." Before Garret could respond, she turned and walked to the door, pausing just before she opened it. She glanced over her shoulder, her cold eyes meeting his. "I'll be watching you. Be careful who you trust."

The door clicked shut behind her with a soft finality, leaving Garret in the silence of his office. He stared at the door for a moment, his mind racing as he processed everything Darla had said.

He stood up, his chair scraping against the floor as he walked toward the window. The town lay below him, quiet and unsuspecting. He picked up the phone and quickly dialed. "Hey, it's me, I need you to meet me at my house now."

THE LATE EVENING AIR was sharp and biting as Garret steered his truck down the winding road toward his house. Boone sat in the passenger seat, his nose pressed against the window, watching the world go by with his usual quiet intensity. Garret could see the dim lights of his home up ahead, a welcome sight after a long and exhausting day.

As he pulled into the driveway, he noticed Mallory already standing on the porch. Boone's ears perked up at the sight of her, and as soon as Garret put the truck in park, the dog bounded out of the vehicle with an enthusiastic leap.

"Hey, buddy," Mallory greeted the dog in her usual sweet voice, bending down to offer Boone a treat. She scratched behind his ears as he happily accepted the biscuit, tail wagging like crazy. Then her eyes flicked up to Garret, and the smile on her face softened.

"Hey," Garret replied, stepping out of the truck and heading up the porch steps toward her. Boone had already zoomed ahead and was now waiting impatiently by the door.

Garret grabbed the door handle and opened it, allowing Mallory and Boone to step inside. He flipped on the living room light, the soft glow illuminating the space.

"Make yourself comfortable," he offered, motioning to the couch. He set his keys down on the counter, his thoughts already racing.

Mallory did as he asked, setting her bag down on the chair and placing two coffee cups on the table in front of them. "I thought you might need something to wake you up. You sounded pretty rough when we talked earlier," she said as she settled beside him, handing him one of the cups.

Garret took a long sip from the coffee, feeling the warmth spread through his chest. "Thanks. You're right. It's been a day."

Mallory raised an eyebrow, studying him for a moment. "What happened after I left to have dinner with my mom?" she asked.

Garret sighed, his fingers tapping the side of the mug. He set it down on the table, his jaw tightening. "Darla," he muttered, his voice low, as if just saying her name was enough to make his frustrations boil over. "She came to see me this afternoon. And let me tell you, she was as calm and calculated as ever. But the things she said—" He rubbed his temples as if trying to push out the memories. "She's been working hard to slow down this investigation, Mallory. She kept pressing about the Maynard family, asking why we were looking into them. It was almost like she knew too much, like she was already one step ahead of us."

Mallory's brow furrowed, and her lips pressed together in a tight line. "What do you think that means?" she asked, her voice steady.

"I think someone's leaking information," Garret muttered, his fingers curling into fists. "I can't shake the feeling that someone in my department is feeding Darla intel about our moves, and that's why she's trying to slow us down. She's trying to keep us from getting too close to the truth."

Mallory's expression darkened as she processed the implications of what Garret had just said. "Do you have anyone in mind?" she asked carefully.

Garret leaned back in the chair, staring at the ceiling for a moment as he thought. "Well, I know it's not you. And it's definitely not Josie. She's been working her ass off on this case, just like Ryan. Maggie wouldn't do it either. So that leaves..."

He trailed off, his thoughts spinning.

"It has to be someone who's been in the department for a while, someone with knowledge of the inner workings. Someone who's been here long enough to know who's investigating what."

Mallory nodded, her expression thoughtful. "So that rules out the newer deputies. We're looking for someone with deeper ties to the department."

Garret's mind raced, running through the faces of his team. "I don't know. I need to think this through."

The silence hung in the air for a few moments before Garret broke it again, his voice thick with frustration. "I just—I feel like we're being watched. Every step we take, someone's right behind us."

Mallory placed a reassuring hand on his shoulder. "We'll figure it out, Garret. You don't have to do this alone."

Garret gave her a small, tight smile. "I know. But it's not just about me. We're all in this together, and if there's someone in the department working against us..." He trailed off, the weight of the thought sinking in. After a long pause, Garret finally stood up. "I'm going to call Ryan and Josie. We need to talk to them. We need to figure out who's behind this."

The phone rang a few times before Ryan answered. "Sheriff? What's going on?"

"I need you and Josie to meet me at my house," Garret said, his voice firm. "We need to talk."

There was a pause on the other end of the line. "Got it. We'll be there as soon as we can."

Garret ended the call and turned to Mallory. "They're on their way. We'll figure this out, one way or another."

Soon enough, Ryan and Josie arrived at Garret's house, both of them looking slightly on edge.

"Garret, Mallory," Ryan said, his voice low. "What's going on?"

Josie gave a quick glance around the room. "Is everything okay?"

Garret took a deep breath and motioned for them to sit down. As they gathered around the table, he explained everything he'd discussed with Darla earlier, from her attempts to stall the investigation to the suspicion that there was a mole in the department. He explained how Darla's focus on the Maynard family had tipped him off that someone had access to their investigation.

"We need to figure out who it is," Garret said bluntly. "Someone's been feeding Darla information, and I think it's one of us."

The room fell silent as everyone processed the weight of Garret's words.

Josie was the first to speak up. "But it can't be any of us, right? I mean, we've all been working our asses off."

Garret nodded. "I know. That's why I'm not pointing fingers at any of you."

Ryan crossed his arms, clearly concerned. "Then who do you think it is?"

Garret ran a hand through his hair. "I don't know. I think we need to look at Deputy Ben Stockard. He's been with the department for years, but he's never quite fit in with the rest of us. And he's got ties to Darla. I think he's the one we've been looking for."

Ryan's eyes widened. "You're serious?"

"I am," Garret replied. "We need to keep an eye on him."

MALLORY'S PHONE RANG just as she was stepping out of her SUV, the low hum of the engine still echoing in her ears. She glanced at the caller ID, seeing Dana Gaines' name flash on the screen. It had been a while since the tech analyst had provided them with anything of interest, but Mallory knew Dana's ability to dig into the past was invaluable. She swiped to answer, shifting her weight from foot to foot as she waited for Dana to speak.

"Mallory," Dana's voice came through clear and focused. "I've got more information for you—about Darla Hensley and her family. This might give you some perspective on her, and it could tie into some of what you're dealing with right now."

Mallory felt her pulse quicken. "I'm listening."

Dana's voice took on a more serious tone. "So, Darla Hensley isn't just a product of her own political career. She's got deep family ties in Blackwater Ridge that go way back—ties that connect her to some unsavory parts of town history. Her father, Matthew Hensley, was the mayor for two terms, from the late 90s to the early 2000s. Matthew wasn't exactly a model citizen, though. From what I've dug up, he was involved in some controversial zoning decisions that didn't sit well with the community, but they certainly lined his pockets and those of his closest allies. Land deals, public projects—nothing outright illegal, but let's just say there were a lot of backroom deals that benefited people who could afford to keep things quiet."

Mallory frowned. She'd suspected there was more to Darla's rise in politics than met the eye. "And what about her grandfather? You mentioned he was involved too?"

Dana hesitated for a moment, as if considering how to phrase her next words. "Her grandfather, Benjamin Hensley, was mayor before Matthew—back in the late '80s and early '90s. He had a reputation for being a tough, no-nonsense type. But the thing that stands out the most about Benjamin Hensley, Darla's grandfather, is his connection to the Maynard family. It wasn't just political—it was personal, too. Benjamin Hensley and Thomas Maynard, a member of the Maynard family who was influential in the 1980s, were not only political allies but also partners in several land deals in Blackwater Ridge. These deals were often shrouded in mystery, with little documentation to show what truly transpired behind closed doors.

"It's believed that Hensley and Maynard worked together on various projects that involved land development near the church on the ridge. Though the specifics of these deals have been lost to time, there were whispers that the Maynards were involved in something far darker—an unsettling connection to the old church's history. Some suggested that Benjamin Hensley and Thomas Maynard were working in tandem to secure land that had once been part of Silas Bennington's domain—and that there may have been an intention to revive certain rituals or traditions tied to the church's original purpose.

"Hensley's involvement with the Maynards has always been a point of speculation, particularly because there are few records of these dealings, and the Hensley family has always been remarkably tight-lipped about their past. But the connection is undeniable, and while Benjamin Hensley was known for his political maneuvering, it's clear that he was more than willing to make deals with the Maynards—deals that may have had sinister implications for Blackwater Ridge."

Mallory leaned against the side of her truck, trying to steady her thoughts. "Jesus. You're good at your job. How'd you get that much information?"

Dana chuckled. "Online archives. Census records. And other methods. I can't give away all my secrets."

"Okay. So, let me get this straight. The mayor's great-great-grandfather Samuel Hensley was directly involved with Bennington?"

"That's right," Dana replied. "Samuel Hensley was a reverend, but not just any preacher. He was one of Bennington's closest allies, and they shared more than just business interests. Supposedly, Samuel Hensley was part of the group that helped Bennington establish the church on the ridge—possibly even helping to fund it. Some even say Samuel Hensley was involved in the darker side of the church's practices—rituals, ceremonies, whatever you want to call it. But of course, there's no solid evidence. Just rumors. Still, I don't think it's a coincidence that Darla has climbed the political ladder as fast as she has, given her family's connections."

Mallory's brow furrowed, her fingers tightening around the phone. "This is a lot to take in. Are you saying Darla could be involved in some of the same things her family was connected to years ago?"

Dana paused before responding. "Not directly, maybe. But I wouldn't put it past her to use those same connections. Her political career is built on the Hensley name, and she's made a lot of promises to the people in Blackwater Ridge—promises she may not have the power to keep without help from old allies. If her family's history with the Maynards and Benningtons is any indication, Darla knows exactly how to manipulate those in power."

Mallory's thoughts swirled. She had suspected that Darla's rise to mayor wasn't entirely clean, but now the pieces were starting to form a picture that was darker than she had imagined. "And the political stuff... are there any scandals or things she might have hidden from her time in office?"

Dana's tone lowered as she delved into the darker side of Darla's past. "There's one particularly shady thing that came up when I was digging into her father's time in office. Matthew Hensley had a business associate—someone in real estate—who went missing under strange circumstances. The whole thing was swept under the rug, but there were reports that Matthew had been involved in some illegal land acquisitions, including using his influence as mayor to seize properties from struggling homeowners for far less than their worth. There were rumors that the missing associate had been going to the press with evidence of these deals before he disappeared. But the case was never solved, and as far as I can tell, no one has ever truly looked into it again."

"Do you think Darla's aware of this?" Mallory asked, feeling her blood run cold.

"Of course she's aware," Dana said flatly. "It's a family business, and Darla's been groomed to take over for years. She may not have been directly involved in those illegal activities, but she's certainly benefited from them. The Hensley name carries a lot of weight in Blackwater Ridge, and Darla's used that to climb the ranks of local politics. She's made herself indispensable to the town by promising progress and keeping the local businesses happy, all while maintaining close ties to the old guard—the ones who have their hands in the dirt."

Mallory felt a sense of dread settle in her stomach. "So, you're telling me Darla's not just a politician—she's part of a long line of power and influence that's been tied to the darkest corners of Blackwater Ridge. And she's using that history to maintain control?"

"That's exactly what I'm saying," Dana replied. "The Hensley family's history with the Maynards and Benningtons isn't something Darla can afford to ignore. I'm sure she's kept ties with some of the old family friends who are still involved in the land deals and politics, and I wouldn't be surprised if she's using those connections to manipulate the town even further."

Mallory took a deep breath. "Thanks, Dana. This is huge. You've given me more than enough to go on. I'll be in touch if I need anything else."

"You got it," Dana said. "Stay careful, Mallory."

Chapter Thirteen

The early morning darkness was still thick when a loud knock shattered Mallory's fragile grip on sleep. She groaned, rolling over and burying her face in her pillow in protest. The knock came again, more insistent this time. She threw back the covers with a huff and stomped to the door, her bare feet slapping against the cold hardwood floor.

"Who is it?" she barked, her voice heavy with irritation.

"Mal, it's me." Garret's voice came through the door, calm but firm.

Frowning, she unlocked the door and pulled it open. His hair was tousled, and his face was lined with a weariness that matched her own. He held out a steaming cup of coffee like a peace offering.

"Garret, what on earth are you doing here at four in the morning?" she asked, her groggy tone thick with annoyance as she stepped aside to let him in.

"I'm sorry, I know it's early," he said, his voice apologetic as he handed her the coffee. "But we need to talk."

Mallory took the cup with a scowl, the warmth seeping into her cold hands. "This couldn't wait a few more hours?" she muttered, taking a long sip of the coffee and savoring its bitter, life-giving heat.

Garret chuckled softly at her disgruntled demeanor. "I don't think so. It's about the journal Maggie gave you, her grandmother's journal."

Mallory blinked, her mind slowly catching up. "Maggie said it wasn't much, just some personal notes. I doubt it'll help."

"Maybe," Garret said, his expression intent. "But Maggie doesn't do things without a reason. If she gave it to us, there's something in there we need to see."

Mallory sighed, setting her coffee down on the table with a resigned thud. She crossed the room to her bag, rummaging through its contents until she pulled out a worn leather journal. The initials **E.L.** were embossed on the front in faded gold, the cover cracked and weathered with age.

She flipped it open, revealing a delicate inscription written in flowing, old-fashioned handwriting. Clearing her throat, she read aloud:

"'To whomever reads this, this was my mother, Esther Langton's journal. What you will find in these pages is the story of one woman's journey of survival. While reading this, please keep an open mind, as some entries may seem... unusual. Elizabeth Susannah Whitaker.'"

Mallory glanced up, her brow furrowing.

"Elizabeth Susannah Whitaker... Susannah, like Susannah Fairchild?" Mallory asked.

Garret nodded, his brow lifting in curiosity. "That's not exactly a common spelling. Could it be a connection?"

"It's possible," Mallory said, flipping through the yellowed pages. She stopped when an entry caught her eye. The date scrawled at the top was November 1, 1893.

"Listen to this," she said, reading the entry. "'Susannah is gone. My dearest and truest friend has vanished, and my heart is heavy with sorrow. She was last seen yestereve, following the evening service, and none have beheld her since. Father insists it is the will of the Lord, that she hath been chosen for some higher purpose. Yet, I cannot bring myself to believe him.

"'There was fear in her countenance the night prior—the quiver of her hands as she clasped mine betrayed her distress. In hushed tones, she confided in me that she had chanced upon Father and Mr. Maynard speaking in secrecy, her name passing betwixt them. She scarce dared to utter it, but she claimed they spoke of the cellar beneath the church, a place forbidden to me all my life.

"'A dreadful unease has taken root in my breast. I fear she is even now imprisoned within that wretched place, frightened and alone. I long to seek her out, yet Father watches me with a wary eye. Though he speaks not of it, I am certain he perceives my suspicion. Should I find means to enter the cellar, I shall set down here all that I discover. Perchance, these words shall serve some purpose, if ever they be found.'"

Mallory's voice trailed off, the weight of the words hanging in the air like a dense fog.

Garret leaned forward, his jaw tightening. "She's talking about a cellar beneath the church," he said. "A place they kept hidden."

Mallory nodded, her fingers tracing the edges of the brittle page. "Let me see if there's more." Before she began to read, a thought hit her, "Oh my gosh, Garret!"

"What?"

"I just realized that Silas Bennington had a daughter named Ester." He looked at her, not quite following where she was going. She continued, "Esther Langston was Esther Bennington. Elizabeth Whitaker is Maggie's grandmother, which means that Esther Bennington was Maggie's great-grandmother."

Garret looked confused, "Why wouldn't Maggie tell us that?"

Mallory shrugged, "I don't know. Maybe she didn't think it was relevant. Or maybe she doesn't like having her name tied with the Bennington name."

Mallory turned the page, her eyes scanning the faded script until another entry stood out. The date was two weeks later, November 15, 1893.

"Here's another entry," Mallory said. "'I have seen it now. The cellar beneath the church is no common place, but a prison—a wretched den of shadows and despair. Iron chains are fastened to the walls, and the air is thick with a stench so vile it clings to the very skin. Father and Mr. Maynard name it the sanctum, yet there is naught of holiness within its depths.

"'Last eve, I concealed myself upon the stair and bore witness as they led Susannah below. She was frail, scarcely able to stand. Father spoke of purification, yet his words rang cold and hollow. They bound her to the altar at the room's center, and the others gathered about, murmuring incantations in a tongue most unnatural to mine ear.

"'These rites are not of God. They speak of summoning power, of unlocking the earth's forbidden secrets. I know not what they seek, only that it is wicked. I tremble for Susannah, and I tremble for myself. Should they discover what I have seen, I do not doubt they would see me silenced.'"

Garret swore under his breath, his fists clenching. "They were keeping people down there. Performing rituals on them. Holy shit. Maggie knew about this the whole time. You don't think she's involved in this cult, do you?"

"I don't think so," Mallory replied. "If she was, then why would she give us this book?"

"Keep going," Garret urged.

Mallory hesitated, but her fingers turned the page once more. The final entry that caught her eye was dated nearly a month later: December 12, 1893.

"'I can no longer abide in silence. Susannah is gone, and Father speaks not her name. He claims she hath been delivered, but I know the truth. I beheld the blood upon the altar that morning. I saw Mr. Maynard bearing away some dreadful thing, swathed in cloth, his visage as pale as death itself.

"'The cellar is a place of unspeakable horror. Others now languish in its depths—wayward travelers, strangers who pass through town and are never seen again. The rituals persist, the shadows grow ever deeper. Father proclaims it to be for the glory of the church, yet I see only avarice and cruelty.

"'I must flee, else I shall surely meet the same fate as Susannah. This journal is my sole hope, the only means by which the truth may endure. Should these words find you, know that I resisted. I strove to fight, but the darkness was greater than I.'"

Mallory closed the journal with trembling hands, her face pale.

"Esther knew what was happening, but she couldn't stop it. They were using the cellar for their rituals, and people were dying because of it."

Garret nodded, his expression grim. "And if there's any chance that cellar still exists, we need to find it. It might hold the answers we're looking for."

THE OLD CHURCH LOOMED in the pale light of dawn, its weathered wood and crumbling steeple casting long, jagged shadows over the overgrown yard. The air was damp and heavy, carrying the scent of rotting leaves and earth. Mallory stood at the edge of the clearing, the journal clutched tightly in her gloved hands.

Mallory turned the leather-bound journal toward Garrett, tapping the faded map sketched on one of its pages. "Esther's description matches this spot. The cellar should be somewhere beneath the church."

Boone sniffed the ground, his tail wagging uncertainly as he padded forward. Josie and Ryan flanked Garret, their faces tense but alert.

"Let's move," Garret said, leading the group up the broken steps and through the arched double doors.

Inside, the church was deathly silent, the air thick with an oppressive stillness. Dust motes swirled in the beams of light streaming through cracked stained-glass windows, painting the warped wooden pews in muted colors. The altar stood at the far end, its white cloth yellowed with age and marred by stains too dark to identify.

Boone let out a low whine, his nose working furiously as he tugged at his leash.

"What is it, boy?" Mallory asked, kneeling beside him.

The dog's ears perked up, and he pulled toward the altar. Mallory exchanged a glance with Garret, who nodded.

"Check it out," Garret said, gesturing toward the front.

They moved as a group, their footsteps echoing on the creaking floorboards. Boone stopped at the base of the altar, sniffing furiously at the floor. He pawed at a spot near the corner, his claws scraping against the wood.

"Looks like he's onto something," Josie said, stepping closer.

Ryan knelt beside Boone, running his fingers along the floorboards. "There's a seam here," he said. "Could be a trapdoor."

Garret crouched beside him, pulling out a pocketknife. He slid the blade into the seam and pried upward. The wood groaned in protest before giving way with a sharp crack. A hidden door swung open, revealing a set of narrow stone steps descending into darkness.

The group stared down into the black void, the air wafting up from below, cold and musty.

"Well," Mallory said, her voice steady despite the unease gnawing at her stomach, "this looks promising."

Garret turned on his flashlight, the beam cutting through the darkness. "Stay close. Boone, you're with me."

The group descended cautiously, the narrow steps slick with moisture. Boone moved ahead of Garret, his tail wagging nervously as he sniffed the air. The walls were rough stone, damp and cold to the touch. The further they went, the thicker the air seemed to grow, heavy with the scent of decay.

At the bottom of the stairs, the space opened into a low-ceilinged room. The flashlight beams danced across the walls, revealing rusted chains bolted into the stone and dark stains smeared across the floor. A wooden table sat in the center of the room, its surface scarred and pitted.

Josie gagged, covering her mouth with her hand. "What the hell is this place?"

"Looks like Esther was telling the truth," Garret said grimly.

"This might have been the place Sadie was talking about," Ryan said glancing around the area.

Mallory moved to the table, scanning its surface. Deep grooves were carved into the wood, forming symbols she couldn't immediately recognize. She took out her phone and snapped a photo, the flash briefly illuminating the room.

Boone barked suddenly, his nose pressed to the far corner of the room.

"What is it, boy?" Garret asked, moving toward him.

Boone pawed at the ground, letting out another sharp bark. Garret shone his flashlight in the direction Boone was pointing, revealing a pile of torn fabric partially buried beneath a layer of dust and debris.

Mallory stepped closer, her breath catching as she recognized the pattern on the fabric. It was a floral dress, faded and torn, with a large dark stain near the hem.

"That's Lila's dress," Josie whispered, her voice trembling.

Mallory knelt beside the dress, carefully pulling it free. Beneath it, she found a scattering of personal items: a broken bracelet, a pair of earrings, and a small leather-bound notebook. She opened the notebook, her eyes scanning the neatly written entries.

"I think this was Lila's."

Garret's jaw tightened, and he reached for his radio. "We need to secure this place and call in a forensics team. Whatever happened here, we've got evidence now."

Ryan nodded, his face pale as he glanced around the room. "This place... it's like something out of a nightmare."

Mallory stood, holding the notebook tightly in her hands. "We need to keep looking. If there's more evidence here, we have to find it."

The group spread out, their flashlights probing the shadows. Mallory moved toward the far wall, where a crude wooden door hung ajar. She pushed it open, revealing a smaller room beyond. The walls were lined with shelves, each one filled with jars and vials coated in a thick layer of grime.

"What is this?" she muttered, her flashlight beam sweeping across the shelves. The jars were filled with strange substances—dried herbs, powders, and what looked disturbingly like bone fragments.

Garret appeared behind her, his flashlight joining hers. "That definitely looks like ritualistic stuff. Maybe this was where they kept their supplies."

Mallory nodded, her stomach churning as she examined the contents of the room. "We need to document all of this. Every detail could be important."

Boone barked again from the main room, drawing their attention. Garret and Mallory hurried back to find Josie crouched near a crack in the wall, her flashlight aimed at the narrow opening.

"There's something back here," Josie said, her voice tight.

Garret leaned in, peering through the crack. "Looks like another chamber. Ryan, help me move this."

Together, the two men pushed against the stone, the wall shifting slowly under their combined strength. With a grinding sound, the crack widened, revealing a hidden doorway.

The chamber beyond was smaller, its walls etched with more of the strange symbols they had seen earlier. In the center of the room was a stone altar, its surface stained and worn.

Mallory's flashlight beam caught something on the floor beside the altar—a small, gold locket. She picked it up carefully, her breath catching as she opened it. Inside was a tiny photograph of a young woman with bright eyes and a radiant smile.

"It's Lila," she said softly, holding the locket up for the others to see.

Josie's eyes filled with tears, and she turned away, her shoulders shaking. Garret placed a hand on her shoulder, his expression heavy with shared grief.

"We've got what we need," Garret said after a moment. "Let's get out of here and call in the team."

BACK AT THE SHERIFF'S office, the air was thick with a mixture of exhaustion and determination. The group had returned after securing the site for forensics. Mallory leaned against the edge of Garret's desk, her arms crossed tightly over her chest, as Boone lay sprawled at her feet, his tail thumping lightly against the floor whenever someone walked by.

Ryan was seated at his desk, his fingers flying over the keyboard as he worked on pulling up property records. Josie leaned over his shoulder, her brow furrowed in concentration. Garret stood by the window, sipping coffee that had long since gone cold.

Mallory broke the silence. "We need to know who owns that land. Someone has to be responsible for it, and whoever it is might have answers—or know more than they're letting on."

Ryan nodded without looking up, his focus locked on the screen. "I'm already on it. Pulling up the county records now."

Josie straightened, glancing at Garret. "If it's abandoned, it might not lead to anything. But if it's still tied to someone, that could be a break."

"It has to be tied to someone," Mallory said, her voice firm. "That church didn't just appear out of nowhere, and the fact that it's still standing means someone maintained the property, even if just on paper. If you can't figure it out, I can call Dana," Mallory said impatiently.

Ryan clicked through a few more pages, then leaned back in his chair, his eyes narrowing. "Got it," he said.

Garret turned from the window, setting his mug down on the desk. "Who owns it?"

Ryan's mouth pressed into a thin line. "The Maynard family."

"The Maynards?" Josie echoed, disbelief coloring her tone. "As in Caleb Maynard's family?"

Ryan nodded. "The church property is part of their estate. It connects to their main property by about two acres of forested land. According to the records, it became theirs in 1898, right after Silas Bennington disappeared. It looks like the land was deeded over to the Maynard family at that time—probably part of some arrangement or inheritance."

Mallory frowned. "So, the Maynards have technically owned that property for over a century, and no one thought to question it? No one thought it was strange that it ended up in their hands after Bennington vanished?"

Garret sighed, rubbing a hand over his face. "This town doesn't question much when it comes to the old families. The Maynards have been a fixture here forever, just like the Benningtons. People probably assumed it was some kind of agreement between them—family business."

"But if they've owned it all this time," Josie said, "then they had to know about that cellar. *Someone* had to know."

Ryan clicked through a few more screens, scanning the documents. "There's nothing in the records about any structures on the property other than the church. No mention of a cellar, no outbuildings, nothing. It's like that part of the property doesn't exist on paper."

"Convenient," Mallory muttered.

Garret stepped forward, his expression grim. "This ties Caleb Maynard into things a lot more directly. If his family owns that land and it's tied to Bennington, we need to question him. But we're going to need a warrant to get anything out of him. He's not just going to hand over information willingly."

Josie shifted uncomfortably. "Do you think Caleb knows anything? He's always come across as a little off, but that doesn't mean he's involved."

Garret's eyes darkened. "Caleb's a wildcard. He's been on our radar for years—nothing we could ever pin on him, but he's connected to a lot of shady dealings. Now we know his family owns the land where we found evidence of Lila. That's enough for me to want to dig deeper."

Mallory straightened. "We don't just need a warrant for Caleb. We need access to every part of that property. If the church and the cellar are connected to something larger, there could be more evidence hidden in the woods or on their main property."

Ryan nodded. "I can draft a request for the warrant, but we'll need solid probable cause. Finding Lila's things in the cellar is a start, but we need to make it airtight."

Mallory thought for a moment, then walked over to Garret's desk, pulling out the locket they had found. She held it up. "This, plus her dress and notebook, should be enough to link the site to her disappearance. It is directly connected to Caleb's family property. That's a strong connection."

Garret took the locket, turning it over in his hand. His jaw tightened as he stared at the small photograph inside. "It's more than strong. It's personal now. We'll get the warrant."

Boone let out a soft woof, breaking the tension in the room.

Garret glanced down at the dog, a faint smile tugging at his lips despite the gravity of the situation. "Good work, buddy," he said, giving Boone a scratch behind the ears.

Josie crossed her arms, her expression thoughtful. "If we're going after Caleb, we need to be ready. He's not the type to roll over easily, and if he knows anything, he'll fight to keep it buried."

"Let him try," Garret said firmly. "We've got enough to start unraveling this, and we're not stopping now."

Mallory nodded, her determination matching his. "We'll get the warrant. And then we'll get answers."

Ryan tapped a few final keys on his keyboard, printing out the property records. He handed them to Garret, who scanned them quickly before folding them into his pocket.

"I'll get the paperwork started," Ryan said, standing. "With everything we found, it shouldn't take long to get approval."

Garret clapped him on the shoulder. "Good. Let's move fast. The sooner we get access, the better."

Mallory glanced at the clock on the wall. It was barely past noon, but the weight of the day's discoveries made it feel much later. "We've got a long road ahead," she said. "But at least we're heading in the right direction."

THE ROOM WAS LIT ONLY by the faint flicker of a single candle set atop a wooden table. The faint scent of wax and smoke lingered in the air, mixing with the musk of old wood. One figure sat at the table, leaning forward, their hands steepled beneath their chin. A phone lay flat on the table, speaker active, as a voice crackled from the other end.

"They found it." The voice was low, trembling with restrained panic.

A pause. Then a soft chuckle from the figure at the table, cold and dismissive. "And?"

"What do you mean, *and*? They found the cellar. They know someone was there." The caller's voice grew sharper, more insistent. "They're going to ask for a warrant."

The figure tilted their head, the faintest shadow of a smile tugging at their lips. "They can ask all they like. That doesn't mean they'll get it."

"You don't understand," the caller pressed, the desperation thick in their tone. "They're connecting the dots. The church, the property, the missing women... It's all starting to unravel. If they get a warrant, it's over."

The figure's smile widened, but there was no warmth in it. "No, it's not. The system was designed to work for people like us, remember? Nothing unravels unless I let it."

A shaky exhale echoed over the line. "You can't be sure of that. They're relentless. The sheriff, the agent—they won't stop."

"They will." The words were spoken with quiet, icy confidence. "Because the law isn't on their side. The judge is a loyal friend, and loyalty has its rewards. The request will be denied for lack of evidence or procedural issues—take your pick. They'll hit a wall. And when they do, they'll waste precious time trying to climb over it."

The caller hesitated. "And if they find a way around it? If they—"

"They won't," the figure interrupted, their voice sharp as a blade. "Do you think I haven't accounted for that? Every contingency has been planned for. The more they push, the more tangled they'll become in red tape. Frustration will slow them down, and when the time comes, they'll have nothing but dead ends."

The line was silent for a moment, save for the faint hiss of static. Then, the caller spoke again, their voice quieter now. "You're certain?"

"Yes." The figure's tone was clipped, final. "But you need to stay calm. Panic makes mistakes, and we can't afford those right now. Stick to the plan, and let me handle the rest."

"I still don't like this," the caller murmured. "They're too close. And what about the property? You think they won't figure out who owns it?"

The figure laughed softly, the sound devoid of humor. "They can figure out whatever they like. Ownership is irrelevant. The one who owns it knows nothing. It's a convenient shield, and they won't even realize they're being used."

"But what if—"

"No 'what ifs,'" the figure snapped, their patience thinning. "The moment you start doubting is the moment everything falls apart. Do your part, and I'll do mine. And for the love of everything we've worked for, stop calling me unless it's absolutely necessary."

The caller fell silent, their unease palpable even through the static. Finally, they muttered, "Fine. But if this blows up—"

"It won't." The figure reached for the candle, pinching the flame between their fingers without flinching. The room plunged into darkness. "They won't touch us. They don't even know where to start."

The line went dead with a faint click.

Chapter Fourteen

The sun was setting over Blackwater Ridge, casting a golden hue across the land. Garret's house was nestled in a quiet spot just outside town, the kind of place that felt safe and far removed from the shadows they'd been chasing. Mallory stood on the porch, arms crossed, staring at the horizon. The view was beautiful, but her mind was too tangled in frustration to appreciate it.

The screen door creaked behind her, and she turned as Garret stepped outside, with two steaming mugs in his hands. He offered one to her without a word, and she took it, the warmth a welcome comfort against the evening chill.

"Thanks," she murmured, taking a sip.

Garret leaned against the wooden railing, his expression pensive. "Mallory, we need to talk."

The tone of his voice made her stomach tighten. "That doesn't sound good."

He sighed, rubbing the back of his neck. "It's not. The judge denied our warrant."

Her eyes widened, her grip tightening on the mug. "What? Why?"

"They claimed we didn't have enough evidence to justify it," Garret said, his voice tinged with frustration. "Said our findings in the cellar were 'inconclusive' and that we needed more proof to tie it to anything criminal."

"That's ridiculous!" Mallory snapped, setting her mug down on the railing. "We found blood, Garret. Blood. And not just that—there were chains, signs that someone was being held down there."

"I know," he said softly, meeting her gaze. "I'm just telling you what they said. But there's more."

She arched a brow, waiting.

"The judge who denied the warrant is Judge Lambert," Garret continued. "He's good friends with Darla Hensley—and he was also close with Charles Maynard, Caleb's grandfather."

Mallory's jaw clenched. "So, you're saying this is political. Lambert's protecting them."

Garret nodded grimly. "It sure looks that way."

For a moment, the weight of it all pressed down on her. The pieces were falling into place, and none of it felt like a coincidence. "If they think this is going to stop us, they're wrong," she said, her voice firm.

Garret tilted his head, a small smile tugging at his lips. "I figured you'd say that. What's your plan?"

She smirked, a determined glint in her eyes. "I'm going over their heads. I'll call my boss and request a federal warrant. This is bigger than Blackwater Ridge, Garret. If the locals won't play fair, I'll bring in the big guns."

Garret chuckled softly, but there was admiration in his eyes. "I don't doubt you for a second, Agent Mallory Cole."

For a moment, their eyes met, and the air between them shifted. The weight of their mission faded briefly, replaced by something unspoken. Mallory felt her heart skip, but she quickly cleared her throat, breaking the spell. "I need to make that call," she said, stepping away from the porch railing.

Garret nodded, his gaze lingering on her as she walked inside.

Mallory paced in Garret's cozy living room, the phone pressed to her ear. It rang twice before a familiar voice answered. "Larkin here."

"Richard, it's Mallory," she said quickly.

"Mallory," Larkin's deep voice softened slightly. "What's going on? Is everything okay?"

"Not exactly," she admitted. "We've hit a wall with the investigation. We found a hidden cellar under the church on Blackwater Ridge—chains, bloodstains, the works. But the local judge denied our warrant to search the rest of the property, claiming we don't have enough evidence."

"Let me guess," Larkin said, his tone dry. "This judge has connections to the people you're investigating?"

"Bingo," Mallory replied. "He's close with the mayor, who's tied up in all this, and he was friends with the Maynard family. I think he's protecting them."

There was a pause on the other end of the line. "What do you need from me?"

"A federal warrant," Mallory said. "We can't move forward without one. The evidence we found is enough to raise major red flags. Someone was held in that cellar, Richard. Someone was hurt—or worse."

Larkin exhaled. "Alright. I'll make some calls. This won't be easy—you know how jurisdictional politics can get—but I'll get it done."

"Thank you," she said, relief washing over her.

"You're sure about this, though?" Larkin asked, his voice quieter now. "You're certain this is where the trail leads?"

"I am," she said without hesitation. "And I'm not stopping until we figure out who's behind this."

There was a brief silence, and then Larkin spoke again. "I'll have an answer for you by morning. Stay safe, Mallory. Sounds like you're walking into dangerous territory."

"Thanks, Richard. I will," she said before hanging up.

When Mallory returned to the porch, Garret was still leaning against the railing, his own coffee forgotten beside him. He turned as she stepped out, his brow lifting in question.

"Richard's on it," she said with a small smile. "We'll have our warrant soon."

Garret nodded, a faint smirk playing on his lips. "I never doubted you."

"You're learning," she teased, leaning against the railing beside him.

The golden hues of the sunset had faded into deep purples and blues, the first stars winking into view above them. For a moment, they stood in comfortable silence, the cool night air wrapping around them.

"You know," Garret said softly, breaking the quiet, "this town hasn't seen someone like you in a long time."

Mallory arched a brow, glancing at him. "Someone like me?"

He shrugged, his eyes on the horizon. "Someone who doesn't back down. Someone who's willing to fight for the truth, no matter the cost."

She felt a warmth rise in her chest at his words. "Well, I'm not doing it alone," she said, nudging his arm lightly. "You've been in this fight longer than I have, Garret. You care about this town more than anyone I've met."

He looked at her then, his expression unreadable. "Maybe. But I didn't search the cabin... Shit, I've made so many mistakes."

"Hey. We all make mistakes," Mallory said. "Even me."

"Yeah, well, it's different now. With you here... I don't feel like I'm fighting a losing battle anymore."

Mallory's breath hitched slightly at the sincerity in his tone. She looked away, focusing on the stars instead of the way his gaze made her heart flutter. "We're a team," she said quietly. "And we're going to figure this out. Together."

Garret's lips curved into a small smile. "Yeah. Together."

THE SMELL OF BLEACH and antiseptic filled the sterile air as Mallory and Garret stepped into the hospital lobby. The faint sound of machines mingled with the soft murmur of voices. Mallory adjusted the strap of her shoulder bag, her expression serious as she approached the front desk.

"We're here to see Sadie Harper. Room 212," she said, flashing her badge to the nurse behind the desk.

The nurse nodded. "Second floor, take the elevators on your left. She's stable but still recovering. Don't push her too hard."

Garret nodded his thanks, but his mind was already elsewhere. "Do you think she'll recognize it?" he asked Mallory quietly as they headed for the elevator.

"I hope so," Mallory replied, pressing the button. "We're running out of leads, and if she remembers anything about that place, it could be the break we need."

The elevator doors opened with a soft chime, and they stepped inside. Garret leaned against the wall, glancing at Mallory. She looked tired but focused, her eyes scanning the folder she carried.

"You okay?" he asked.

She glanced up, offering a faint smile. "I'll be better once we figure out who's behind this."

He nodded, the unspoken weight of the case hanging between them.

When they reached Sadie's room, the door was slightly ajar. Inside, a young woman with pale skin and tired eyes lay propped against a stack of pillows. Her dark hair was pulled back, and though she looked fragile, there was a spark of resilience in her gaze.

Beside her stood two people Mallory immediately recognized—Agent Logan Archer and Agent Elizabeth Morgan. Archer was tall and broad-shouldered, his sharp blue eyes scanning the room with practiced ease.

Morgan, in contrast, was petite but no less commanding, her dark hair pulled into a sleek bun.

"Mallory," Archer greeted, his deep voice warm but professional. He extended a hand, which Mallory shook. "Good to see you again."

"Archer," she replied, then turned to Morgan. "Agent Morgan."

"Agent Crane," Morgan said with a nod. Her tone was cool but polite.

Garret cleared his throat, drawing their attention. "Garret Cole," he introduced himself, shaking hands with both agents. "Sheriff of Blackwater Ridge."

"Cole," Archer said with a slight smile. "Heard a lot about you. Thanks for working with us on this."

"Likewise," Garret replied.

After the introductions, Mallory turned her attention to Sadie. "How are you feeling?" she asked gently, pulling up a chair beside the bed.

Sadie shrugged, her fingers fidgeting with the edge of her blanket. "Better, I guess. The doctors said I'll be fine, but..." Her voice trailed off, and she glanced at the agents.

Mallory placed a reassuring hand on her arm. "You're safe now. That's what matters. But we need your help, Sadie. There's something we need you to look at."

Sadie's eyes flicked to Mallory and then to Garret, who pulled a small stack of photos from his jacket pocket. He handed them to Mallory, who laid them on the bed.

"These are from a cellar we found under the old church on the ridge," Mallory explained. "We need to know if you've ever seen this place before."

Sadie hesitated, her hand hovering over the photos. "The church?" she murmured, her voice barely audible.

Mallory nodded. "It's important, Sadie. Anything you can remember could help us."

Sadie's fingers trembled as she picked up the first photo, a close-up of the stone walls lined with chains. Her breathing quickened, and she set it down quickly, as though it burned her fingers. "I—I've been there," she whispered, her voice shaking.

Garret stepped closer, his expression grim. "You're sure?"

She nodded, tears welling in her eyes. "That's where they kept me. I remember the chains... and the smell." She shuddered, clutching the blanket tighter around her shoulders. "It was damp, and there was this noise. Like dripping water."

Mallory leaned forward, her tone gentle but firm. "Was there anyone else with you? Did you see or hear anything that could help us identify who did this?"

Sadie hesitated, her brow furrowing as she struggled to remember. "There were voices," she said finally. "But I couldn't see their faces. They wore masks, like... like animals. I think I heard someone say 'the ridge.'"

Archer exchanged a glance with Morgan, who jotted down notes on a small notepad.

"Did they say anything about why you were taken?" Garret asked, his voice steady.

Sadie shook her head, tears spilling down her cheeks. "No. They just... they just kept saying it had to be done. That it was tradition."

Mallory's jaw tightened, and she placed a comforting hand on Sadie's arm. "You're doing great, Sadie. This helps more than you know."

Sadie sniffled, her gaze darting between them. "Are they still out there?"

"We're doing everything we can to find them," Mallory assured her. "And we will."

After a few more questions, they thanked Sadie and stepped out into the hallway. The tension from the room followed them like a shadow, weighing heavily on their shoulders.

"Well, that confirms it," Archer said, breaking the silence. "The cellar was definitely used to hold at least one of the missing women."

Garret nodded, his expression grim. "And if it's connected to the Maynard property..."

"We need to move fast," Mallory interjected. "Whoever's behind this knows we're getting close."

Morgan crossed her arms, her sharp gaze fixed on Mallory. "Do you think the Maynards are directly involved?"

Mallory hesitated. "I'm not sure yet. But the connection to Silas Bennington and the church is too strong to ignore."

"We're here if you need us," Archer said. "And we can coordinate with your team, Sheriff. This is bigger than any of us thought, but I'm not surprised. Cults are crazy. I've seen it."

Garret met his gaze, the unspoken determination clear between them. "Appreciate that."

As the agents took their place in Sadie's room to stand guard, Mallory and Garret lingered in the hallway.

"You okay?" Garret asked again, his voice softer now that they were alone.

Mallory exhaled, rubbing her temples. "Yeah. It's just... a lot."

He nodded, his hand brushing hers briefly. "We'll get through this. Together."

For a moment, she looked up at him, her tired eyes meeting his. "Thanks, Garret," she said softly.

LATER THAT MORNING, the sun filtered through the dense canopy of trees surrounding the Maynard property, while Mallory, Garret, Ryan, and Josie stood together at the edge of the gravel driveway. Armed with the federal warrant Mallory had fought to secure, they were ready to search the property, an imposing two-story colonial-style home with dark wood siding.

Mallory adjusted her holster as the team approached the front porch. As they reached the steps, the front door creaked open, and a man stepped out. His broad frame filled the doorway, his face twisted in a scowl. His eyes, a piercing gray, locked onto them with an unmistakable mix of anger and suspicion. "What do you want?" he barked.

Garret stepped forward, holding the warrant in his hand. "We have a federal warrant to search your property," he said firmly. "Step aside, Mr. Maynard."

Caleb Maynard's jaw clenched, his fists tightening at his sides. "A warrant? For what?"

Mallory stepped up beside Garret, her expression hard. "We have reason to believe this property may be connected to the disappearance of several women in Blackwater Ridge," she said bluntly.

Caleb's face darkened, his voice rising. "That's absurd! I don't know anything about those women, and they sure as hell aren't on my property!"

"Then you shouldn't have a problem with us taking a look," Garret said evenly. "Step aside, Mr. Maynard. Now."

For a moment, Caleb seemed to weigh his options, his glare shifting between them. Finally, he exhaled sharply and moved out of the doorway, his movements jerky with frustration. "Fine. Do what you need to do. But you're wasting your time."

The house's interior was steeped in history, with antique furniture and faded portraits of grim-faced ancestors hanging on the walls. The faint smell of wood smoke and aged leather lingered in the air.

They moved methodically through the house, splitting into pairs. Mallory and Garret searched upstairs while Ryan and Josie took the first floor.

In one locked room, Garret forced the door open with a firm shove of his shoulder. Inside, they found a collection of ritualistic carvings etched into wooden planks leaning against the walls. Old maps of Blackwater Ridge lay spread across a desk, annotated with symbols she couldn't immediately decipher.

And then there were the journals.

Mallory picked one up, the worn leather cover almost crumbling in her hands. Her fingers traced the name scrawled at the bottom. *Susannah Fairchild*

"This is it," she whispered, flipping through the brittle pages. The text was handwritten, uneven in places as though penned in haste. Her pulse quickened as she skimmed entries about 'cleansing rituals' and 'sacrifices to maintain balance.'"

Garret leaned over her shoulder. "It's disturbing, but it's not proof," he said. "We can seize it, but we'll need more to tie this to anything current."

Mallory nodded, though her jaw tightened in frustration. "Let's keep going."

Downstairs, Ryan called out from the kitchen. "You might want to see this!"

Mallory and Garret hurried down the stairs, finding Ryan and Josie in the pantry. A large rug had been pulled back, revealing a trapdoor with a rusted handle.

Garret crouched down, testing the handle. It groaned in protest, but the trapdoor finally swung open to reveal a dark, narrow staircase descending into the ground. The scent of damp earth and decay wafted up to them,

Garret drew his weapon, the others following suit. "Stay close," he instructed, leading the way down the creaking steps.

At the bottom, their flashlights revealed a small chamber lined with stone walls. Chains hung from iron hooks embedded in the rock, their ends rusted but unmistakable. Scattered on the ground were remnants of clothing, scraps of fabric stained and torn. Mallory's stomach churned at the sight.

Near the far wall, something glinted in the beam of her flashlight. She crouched down and picked up a delicate necklace with a broken chain.

"It's a locket," she murmured. She opened it with trembling fingers. Inside was a tiny photograph of a smiling young woman. "This is Natalie's. I'm sure of it." Mallory glanced down at her own locket, around her neck. "Did all the missing women wear lockets?" she whispered.

Garret stepped closer, placing a steadying hand on her shoulder. "It's something," he said quietly. "This ties her to this place. We'll get the DNA from the bloodstains and the clothing. This isn't over, Mal."

She nodded, her throat tight as she stood.

As they stepped outside onto the porch, the cool air hit them like a wave. Boone trotted over to Garret, his wagging tail offering a moment of comfort in the otherwise grim scene.

But in the shadows of the forest, hidden from view, a figure watched, their fists clenched at their sides, their breath slow and deliberate.

Chapter Fifteen

The harsh fluorescent light reflected off the stark white walls of the interrogation room. Caleb Maynard sat stiffly at the metal table, his arms crossed tightly over his chest. His expression alternated between irritation and exhaustion, his dark eyes glaring at the two figures across from him.

Garret leaned casually against the wall, while Mallory sat directly across from their suspect.

Caleb shifted in his chair. "Let me spell this out for you one more time," he said, his tone clipped. "I've been in Tulsa for the past two months. I was working on a construction project—a skyrise. You can call anyone on my crew and confirm it. Hell, I'll give you my foreman's number. He can vouch for me."

"You can be sure we'll follow up on your alibi, Caleb," Mallory replied, her voice cold and measured. "But this isn't just about where you've been. It's about what we found on your property. The trapdoor in the kitchen pantry? The chamber beneath it? Care to explain that?"

Caleb's jaw clenched, and his fingers curled into fists on the table. "I've told you. I don't know anything about a chamber," he said, his voice rising. "I inherited that property from my grandfather five years ago. I barely spend any time there. Whatever's under that house has nothing to do with me."

Garret pushed off the wall, taking a slow step closer to the table. "So you're saying your grandfather is the one who put chains down there? Fine. But Natalie Baxter's locket was found in that chamber, Caleb. She's only been missing for a few days. Care to explain how that ended up there if you've been in Tulsa this whole time?"

A flicker of unease crossed Caleb's face. "I don't know how that necklace got there," he said firmly. "Look, the property's remote. It wouldn't be hard for someone to break in and use it without me knowing. I don't live there full-time. It's just a place I inherited, and I haven't done much with it."

Mallory's fingers tapped rhythmically against the table, her eyes narrowing. "So, you're saying someone just stumbled onto your property and decided to use it to hide a missing woman?" she asked. "And they just happened to know about a trapdoor and a chamber beneath your kitchen? That's convenient, don't you think? I saw no signs of a break-in."

"I keep the house locked when I'm not there," Caleb snapped. "But locks can be picked. Or maybe my grandfather left a key lying around somewhere. I don't know!"

Garret reached into the folder he held and slammed a leather-bound journal onto the table. The impact made Caleb flinch. "How do you explain this, then?" Garret demanded. "We found it upstairs, along with books on the occult. Been hosting any rituals lately, Mr. Maynard?"

"Rituals?" Caleb's voice rose incredulously. "You're insane! I don't know anything about that!" He turned his glare to Mallory. You're accusing me of things I didn't do!"

Mallory leaned forward, her voice icy. "This isn't just about accusations, Caleb. This journal," she said, tapping the cover, "contains symbols associated with Silas Bennington. Your family's history is tied to his 'church' and its practices. Either you're involved, or you've been ignoring what's happening on your property."

Caleb's shoulders sagged slightly as he exhaled a sharp breath. "I've heard the stories about Bennington and the ridge. I want nothing to do with any of that," he said bitterly. "If someone's been using my property for whatever this is, then I'll let you search the place again. I don't want this hanging over my head any more than you do."

Garret folded his arms across his chest, studying Caleb closely. "We'll hold you to that," he said. "But until we're satisfied, you're not leaving Blackwater Ridge. If you're as innocent as you say, you won't have a problem with us digging deeper into your family's past."

Caleb's lips pressed into a thin line, but he nodded reluctantly. "Fine. I'll cooperate however I can."

Mallory stood, sliding the journal back into the folder. "We'll see, Caleb," she said, her voice cold. "For your sake, I hope you're telling the truth."

Outside the interrogation room, Mallory and Garret walked side by side down the hallway, their footsteps echoing in the quiet.

Garret broke the silence first. "What do you think?"

Mallory glanced at him, her brow furrowed. "I think he knows more than he's letting on. Whether he's directly involved or just willfully ignorant, his family's tied to this."

Garret nodded. "He's too quick to shift the blame. And his story about not knowing what's in that house doesn't sit right with me."

They reached the exit, the crisp evening air hitting them as they stepped outside. Mallory paused, her hand resting on the strap of her bag. "We need to dig deeper," she said. "There's something in his past—his family's past—that's the key to all of this. We just need to figure out what."

Garret looked at her, his expression thoughtful. "We'll figure it out, Mallory. One step at a time."

She met his gaze. "Thanks, Garret," she said softly.

He nodded, a small smile playing at the corners of his mouth. "Anytime."

THE SMALL CABIN SAT nestled deep in the woods, nearly swallowed by the shadows of towering oaks and pines. The windows were shuttered, and a faint glow leaked through the cracks in the boards. Inside, two figures sat at a rickety wooden table, their faces barely visible in the dim, flickering light of a single kerosene lamp.

The taller of the two paced back and forth, their boots thudding softly against the creaky floorboards. Their movements were sharp and agitated, their hands curling into fists at their sides. "They were on the property," they muttered, their voice low and tight.

The second figure remained seated, their posture rigid as they watched the other pace. "We knew this would happen eventually," they replied.

"Not like this!" The taller figure spun around, their voice rising. "A federal warrant? They've got a damn warrant to search the house! Do you know what that means? They're not just poking around anymore—they're digging. And if they dig too deep—"

"They won't find anything."

The taller figure stopped pacing, turning to glare at their companion. "You don't know that. The chamber under the pantry—that's not just some random hole in the ground. If they put the pieces together, we're screwed."

The seated figure leaned forward, their elbows resting on the table, their fingers steepled under their chin. "They won't find the other chamber," they said finally. "It's too well hidden. Even if they suspect it exists, they don't know where to look. And as for the rest... we've taken precautions."

"Precautions?" The taller figure let out a harsh laugh. "Like leaving behind journals filled with occult symbols? Like chains hanging in the damn cellar? How is that taking precautions?"

"That was never supposed to be there when they found it," the seated figure admitted, their tone darkening. "It was a mistake. One that won't happen again."

The taller figure threw their hands up in frustration. "A mistake? That's what you're calling it now? That mistake is going to get us caught!"

The seated figure's voice dropped to a dangerous whisper. "Calm down. Panicking won't fix anything. What's done is done. Now, we need to focus on damage control."

The taller figure's breathing was heavy, their chest rising and falling as they tried to rein in their emotions. They sank into a chair across from their companion, running a hand through their hair. "What if they come back?" they asked, their voice quieter now.

"They will," the seated figure said without hesitation. "They're like dogs with a bone. But that doesn't mean we can't stay ahead of them."

The taller figure frowned, their fingers drumming anxiously against the table. "We're running out of places to hide things. If they find the other chamber, or worse, the tunnel—"

"They won't," the seated figure interrupted sharply. "We've taken steps to ensure that. And as for the tunnel, it's already been sealed off. Even if they find the entrance, they'll think it's just an old cave-in."

The taller figure didn't look convinced. "And what about the Maynard boy? What if he talks?"

The seated figure smirked, though it was a cold and humorless expression. "Caleb Maynard is more useful to us than he knows. He's a convenient distraction—a scapegoat. Let the agents chase their tails trying to pin this on him. By the time they realize he's not involved, it'll be too late."

"And if he figures out what's really going on?"

"Then he becomes a liability," the seated figure said bluntly. "And we deal with liabilities."

The taller figure's gaze dropped to the table, their jaw tightening. "This wasn't supposed to happen like this. We were careful. We planned everything—"

"Plans change," the seated figure interrupted. "And you need to adapt, or you'll fall apart. You know what's at stake here. If we fail..."

The taller figure's eyes flicked upward, meeting their companion's. For a moment, fear flashed across their face.

"We won't fail," the seated figure said firmly, their voice cold and steady. "We've come too far to let it fall apart now."

The taller figure hesitated, then nodded slowly. "What do we do about the agents?"

The seated figure leaned back in their chair. "Crane and Cole are a problem, I'll admit. They're persistent, and they're starting to piece things together. But persistence can be a weakness. All we have to do is give them just enough to keep them chasing the wrong leads."

"And if they get too close?"

The seated figure's eyes narrowed. "Then we remind them why some stones are better left unturned."

Finally, the taller figure stood, their movements slower now, more deliberate. "You'd better be right about this," they said quietly.

"I am," the seated figure replied without hesitation.

The taller figure lingered for a moment, then turned and walked to the door. As they opened it, a gust of cool night air swept into the cabin, carrying with it the faint rustle of leaves and the distant call of an owl.

"Keep your head," the seated figure called after them. "We've weathered storms before. This one will pass, too."

The taller figure didn't respond, stepping out into the darkness and pulling the door shut behind them.

Alone in the cabin, the seated figure let out a slow breath, their steepled fingers tapping rhythmically against their chin. Their gaze drifted to a small, locked chest on the floor beside the table. Inside lay the secrets they had worked so hard to protect—the truths that could unravel everything if they fell into the wrong hands.

They reached down and placed a hand on the chest, their grip tightening. "No one's finding out," they muttered to themselves. "Not now. Not ever."

Outside, the wind picked up, rattling the shutters and shaking the trees. Somewhere in the distance, a figure watched the cabin from the shadows, their presence hidden by the darkness.

MALLORY SAT ALONE AT the long, polished conference room table, surrounded by the items recovered from the Maynard house. The stack of papers, photographs, and artifacts felt overwhelming, yet her attention kept drifting back to one object: Susannah Fairchild's journal. The leather-bound book sat like a whisper of the past, promising secrets hidden in its faded pages.

She reached out, her fingers brushing the worn cover before carefully opening it. The scent of aged paper rose faintly, and the handwriting—delicate and precise—filled her with an inexplicable sense of foreboding. The front page was simple but haunting:

Property of Susannah Fairchild

Mallory skimmed the first several pages. They were filled with accounts of everyday life in the late 19th century—musings about chores, weather, and fleeting moments of joy. But as she turned the pages, her heart quickened when she reached an entry dated August 7, 1893.

> *Tobias and I passed the afternoon in idle reverie, weaving dreams of a life beyond the confines of Blackwater Ridge. He speaks of great cities, teeming with life, where a man may walk unburdened by the whispers of a small-town preacher or the unrelenting judgment of his father. Reverend Bennington grows ever colder. His gaze, sharp as a blade, seems to pierce my very soul, as though he perceives the depths of my love for Tobias—and with each glance, his loathing burns all the fiercer. Tobias vows we shall leave before long, yet each passing day in this wretched place feels*

a wager against fate. I can but pray the world beyond this forsaken town is gentler than the one we know.

Mallory paused, her fingers hovering over the page. There was a wistfulness in Susannah's words, but also fear. As she read further, a chill crept up her spine.

August 28, 1893

This night, I beheld Reverend Bennington as he truly is. By chance, I happened upon him in the wooded grove near the old church, where he stood encircled by strange symbols, carved deep into the earth. He muttered in a tongue unknown to me, the cadence of his voice unsettling, unnatural. The very air grew thick and stifling, as though some unseen force sought to press the breath from my lungs. The shadows about him stirred though no wind did blow.

I fled before he might lay eyes upon me, yet an unshakable dread lingers still. Tobias will not hear of it—he scoffs at the notion that his father could entangle himself in such unholy rites. Yet I know what I saw.

Reverend Bennington is no servant of God. He is something far more terrible.

Mallory's breath hitched. Her hands trembled slightly as she turned to the next entry.

September 10, 1893

This day, I have come to know a most wondrous truth—I carry Tobias' child. A life quickens within me, a part of him that shall endure, come what may.

When I shared the news, joy illuminated his countenance, yet in his eyes, I glimpsed something else—fear. He knows well the depths of his father's wrath should the truth be revealed. Tobias swears we shall leave before long, that we shall find a place where our child may be raised beyond the reach of Reverend Bennington's shadow.

I am certain the babe is a girl. I feel it deep within my soul. She is hope itself, radiant and unyielding, even amidst the encroaching darkness.

"They were going to escape together," Mallory murmured aloud, her voice breaking the stillness of the room. She turned the page, her heart sinking as she read the date.

October 31, 1893

They came for me this night. Reverend Bennington's men broke into our home whilst my father was absent. They seized me and dragged me to the church, where the Reverend awaited. His words were chilling, spoken with unnerving calm, as he spoke of sacrifices and 'greater purposes.' He knows of the child.

I am now imprisoned in a cold, stone chamber beneath the church. The air is damp and heavy with despair, as though the very walls seek to suffocate me. I cannot say how long I have been confined, but I pray Tobias arrives in time to save me, before it is too late.

Mallory's heart raced. "Did Silas plan to sacrifice Susannah and Tobias' child? His own grandchild?" she whispered, horrified. She turned to the next entry with dread.

November 2, 1893

Tobias came for me, as I had always known he would. My heart leapt at the very sight of him, his countenance steadfast and resolute, as he struggled valiantly to free me from my captors. But Reverend Bennington was not unprepared. Tobias bade me flee, to save myself and the child growing within me, but I could not bring myself to leave him. I watched, helpless, as the Reverend's men fell upon him, their cruel hands and swords quelling the life of the man I loved.

They have told me Tobias met his end at the cliffs—an 'accident,' they say, but I know it to be a lie. Reverend Bennington murdered him. My beloved Tobias is gone, and I remain, alone, locked in this prison of stone.

Mallory's hand flew to her mouth, stifling a gasp. Tears burned her eyes. She had known Tobias died two days after Susannah vanished, but reading how it happened—watching the story unfold through Susannah's words—was unbearable. She turned to another entry.

December 25, 1893

Christmas came and passed in mournful silence. No joy fills this wretched place, no light to pierce the darkness. I am left with naught but the cold, unfeeling stone that binds me, and the ceaseless chants of Reverend Bennington above. He holds me captive, for he believes my child to be the key to some vile and profane ritual. I remain alive only for her.

I speak oft to my child, whispering to her of the day we shall escape, of the day when I shall shield her from this suffering, though it cost me my very life.

Tobias, my beloved, if thy spirit doth hear me, grant me strength to endure.

Sadness engulfed Mallory, but she couldn't stop now. She flipped forward, desperation pushing her toward answers. An entry dated April 25, 1894, caught her attention.

Esther hath come for me. After long months of solitude, she appeared unto me like an angel in the stillness of the night. Her countenance was pale, yet her resolve remained unshaken. She spake of having watched and waited for the appointed hour, when she might act. With great cunning, she slipped past the guards and loosed the bonds that held me in my cell.

I am weak, scarcely able to rise, yet Esther's strength doth not falter. She bore me through the woods, to a place of safety, her quiet assurances the only thing that kept me from slipping into unconsciousness.

I know that I cannot endure much longer. My body is shattered, but there is solace in the knowledge that my child shall have a chance, though I may not live to see it.

Mallory's pulse quickened. Esther had saved Susannah, but at what cost? She turned to the final entry with trembling hands.

April 30, 1894

This shall be my final entry.

The pains have begun, and I know my time draws nigh. My strength is spent, but my heart is filled with peace. I have resolved to name her Hope, for that is what she is—hope born of love, a love stronger than the darkness that sought to rend us apart.

I have entrusted Esther with my last wish: to take Hope far from Blackwater Ridge, to raise her in a land untouched by the evil of Reverend Bennington. She hath vowed to protect Hope with her very life.

I have given Esther my locket, bidding her to keep it until Hope is of age, that she might receive it as I did, passed down from my grandmama. It is a token I wish to hand to her, as a bond between us, a gift of our lineage.

Tobias, I shall soon be with thee. Until that time, I will hold fast to the light we kindled together.

To whomever may find this journal: Remember my daughter. Remember her name. She is the light in this encroaching darkness, the proof that love doth endure, even in the face of the greatest evil.

Beside the final entry was a crude drawing of the locket. Mallory's hand flew to her own neck, where a nearly identical locket rested. Her heart pounded in her chest. She reached for Esther's journal and flipped through it until she came to an entry dated June 23, 1914.

Today hath been a day of great joy, though my heart is heavy with bittersweet memories.

Hope was wed to Harland Winslow this afternoon, beneath the great oak tree at the edge of the meadow.

She was a vision, radiant in her white gown, bathed in the light of the sun. In that moment, she resembled Susannah so closely that it took my breath away. The copper of her hair shone against her dark chestnut locks, just as her mother's had once done. I miss her terribly.

Harland is a good man, and his love for Hope is a love that echoes the affection her father once bore for her mother.

As I watched them exchange their vows, a peace settled upon my soul, a peace I have not known in many years. Hope hath found her happiness, and she shall live a life unburdened by the shadows of our past.

Mallory's wide eyes lifted as the door opened, and Garret walked in. "I have to see my mom," she said, rising from her chair.

Garret frowned. "Mallory, what's wrong?"

She stared at him, her voice shaking. "I think I'm the great-great-granddaughter of Susannah Fairchild and Tobias Bennington's daughter."

Chapter Sixteen

Mallory climbed the steps to her childhood home, each creak beneath her feet a testament to the years the old house had endured. She moved as though in a dream, her mind swirling with questions. Could she truly be connected to Susannah Fairchild? Did Reverend Bennington's blood run through her veins? The thought left her dizzy. She steadied herself against the wooden railing, her fingers brushing over the splintered paint.

As Mallory approached the front door, she noticed it was slightly ajar. The screen door stood closed but unlatched, allowing slivers of light and sound to spill through. Voices carried from inside, low and urgent. She froze, straining to catch the conversation drifting from deeper in the house.

"You need to tell her the truth, Iris," a familiar voice said. "She's going to figure it out anyway."

Mallory's breath caught in her throat. That was Maggie Whitaker. *Why would Maggie be here? And what truth were they talking about?*

Her mother's reply came sharp and defensive. "No. She doesn't need to know. It's too dangerous."

Mallory's heart pounded in her chest. She edged closer, careful to keep her movements quiet. Peering through the screen, she could see into the dimly lit hallway that led to the kitchen. The air inside was thick with the scent of freshly brewed coffee. She hesitated. Listening felt wrong, but the urgency in their voices anchored her in place.

Maggie's tone softened but remained resolute. "Iris, she has my great-grandmother's journal—Esther's journal. She's already seen Susannah's. It's only a matter of time before she pieces it all together. Hope was your great-grandmother. Mallory will realize she's a descendant of Susannah and Tobias."

Iris' response came quickly, her voice tight with frustration. "Why, Maggie? Why did you give her that journal? If you'd just kept it to yourself, she wouldn't have known. She wouldn't have figured it out."

Mallory's pulse quickened. She clutched the doorframe, her knuckles white. Gathering her courage, she pushed the screen door open just enough to step inside. The hinges let out a faint squeak, and the voices in the kitchen fell silent.

The hallway felt longer than it ever had before. Mallory walked toward the kitchen, her shoes making soft, deliberate sounds against the worn wooden floor. When she reached the threshold, she stopped, her heart hammering in her chest.

At the small, round table in the center of the kitchen, Iris Crane and Maggie Whitaker sat across from each other. Forgotten coffee cups rested between them. Iris' face was pale, her expression a mixture of anger and unease. Maggie's features were more composed, but there was a sadness in her eyes that Mallory hadn't seen before.

Both women turned toward her as Mallory stepped into the room. "I'm guessing that was about me," she said, her voice steady despite the turmoil inside her.

Iris' lips parted, but no words came out. Maggie sighed, her shoulders slumping.

"Mallory," Maggie said gently, "we didn't mean for you to overhear."

Mallory crossed her arms, trying to ground herself. "But I did. And now I need to know. Am I really related to Susannah Fairchild? To Tobias Bennington?"

Iris' face darkened, and she turned toward Maggie with a look that could pierce steel. "This is your fault," she spat. "You couldn't leave well enough alone."

"Stop," Mallory said firmly. "I'm here now. No more hiding. I deserve the truth."

Iris stared at her daughter. Finally, she nodded and gestured to the empty chair at the table. "Sit down," she said quietly.

Mallory sat, her knees trembling beneath the table.

"You *are* Susannah's descendant," Iris began. "Her daughter, Hope, was my great-grandmother. That makes you the great-great-granddaughter of Susannah Fairchild and Tobias Bennington."

Hearing it spoken aloud felt like a punch to the gut. Mallory's breath hitched, and she leaned back in her chair. "How?" she asked, her voice barely above a whisper. "How did this stay hidden for so long?"

Iris exchanged a glance with Maggie before answering. "Because it had to be. Susannah's bloodline was in danger the moment Reverend Bennington learned of her pregnancy. Even after his death, his followers... they didn't stop. They believed the child—your ancestor—was part of some prophecy or ritual. Esther risked her life to save Hope. And ever since, our family has done everything we could to protect that secret."

Mallory's head spun. "So, you knew? You've always known?"

Iris hesitated, then nodded. "Yes. But it was safer for you not to know. The less you knew, the less danger you were in."

Maggie added, "I didn't agree with keeping it from you, Mallory. That's why I gave you Esther's journal. You deserve to know where you come from."

Mallory shook her head, her thoughts a jumbled mess. "And what am I supposed to do with this?" she asked. "What does it even mean? Am I in danger *now*?"

"Not if we're careful," Iris said quickly. "But you need to understand why this secret matters. It's not just about protecting you. It's about protecting everything Susannah fought for. Everything she gave her life for."

Mallory's stomach churned. "It all makes sense now—how you ranted about protecting me from evil growing up, how you always wanted to know where I was. Still, I don't even know what to think," she admitted, her voice trembling. "This is too much. How am I supposed to...?"

Her words trailed off as tears welled in her eyes. Maggie reached across the table and grasped Mallory's hand. "Take it one step at a time," she said. "You don't have to have all the answers right now. Just know that you're not alone in this."

Mallory nodded, though her heart felt anything but steady. She looked at her mother, searching for some sign of reassurance. But Iris' face was a mask of worry and regret, and Mallory knew she wouldn't find solace there.

"I need some air," Mallory said abruptly, pushing back her chair and standing.

Iris rose to follow her, but Maggie held up a hand, stopping her. "Let her go," she said quietly. "She needs time."

Mallory stepped out onto the porch, the cool evening air hitting her like a splash of water. She leaned on the porch railing, the rough wood cool beneath her palms as she tried to steady her breathing.

Behind her, the muffled voices of her mother and Maggie continued, rising and falling like waves against the shore. Mallory's heart pounded. Her entire life, she had felt like an outsider in her own family, a puzzle piece that didn't quite fit. Now, the edges of that piece were starting to align.

The creak of the screen door broke her reverie. Iris stepped out, her face shadowed by both the dim light and something deeper—a mix of guilt and fear. For a moment, the two women stood in silence, the tension between them thicker than the humid evening air.

"Mallory," Iris began, her voice softer than Mallory expected. "I didn't want you to know any of this."

Mallory turned to face her, crossing her arms over her chest. "Well, I know now, Mom. And I need to know everything. No more secrets."

Iris hesitated, glancing back toward the kitchen where Maggie remained seated. Finally, she stepped closer, lowering her voice. "Let's sit. This isn't easy to explain."

Mallory followed her mother to the porch swing, the chain groaning softly as they settled in. The rhythmic creak of the swing filled the silence until Iris spoke again.

"The journals Maggie gave you, they're part of your legacy."

Mallory's chest tightened. "Why didn't you tell me?"

Iris sighed. "I've known this my whole life, but knowing comes with danger. Reverend Bennington—Silas—wasn't just a cruel man. He was something darker, something unnatural. That darkness didn't die with him. It lingers, and it's tied to our bloodline."

"Mama, I don't believe in all that supernatural stuff. You call it darkness. But I just call it being an evil man."

"No. There's more to it than that. And just because you don't believe it doesn't mean it's not true. The darkness *is* supernatural, something that comes from curses and rituals, things most people wouldn't believe," Iris said, her voice trembling. "Silas believed he could harness power through sacrifice, and Susannah... she was caught in his madness. That's why she died. And that's why I've tried to shield you from this."

Mallory's pulse quickened. "So, you shielded it from me my whole life because this is more than a history lesson. Is it still happening?"

"I don't know," Iris admitted. "Probably. I know you don't believe in all that. But the sacrifices and the rituals... they worked. They gave people power. And I'm not the only one who believes that, so I've had to be wary of people who would use our bloodline to awaken that darkness again."

From inside, Maggie's voice called out. "Iris, she deserves to know everything." Moments later, Maggie appeared in the doorway, her expression resolute. "The journals don't just tell Susannah's story. They're a warning."

Mallory stood, her frustration bubbling over. "You keep saying I deserve to know everything, but you're feeding me all this in pieces. What aren't you telling me?"

Maggie stepped forward, placing a firm hand on Mallory's shoulder. "Some people in this town believe the blood of Susannah's descendants can unlock something ancient, something dangerous."

"So, you *do* know that this cult shit is still going on," Mallory yelled at her mother.

"Honey, she's just been trying to protect you," Maggie said.

"Protect me from what?" Mallory demanded.

Maggie's gaze didn't waver. "From those who would use you to finish what Silas started."

Mallory took a step back, shaking her head. "This is insane. You're talking about rituals and bloodlines like we're in some kind of horror story. And the crazy thing, is y'all believe it as much as they do. And you've kept it quiet, so you're just as bad as them—even if it you're not performing rituals yourself."

"I know how it sounds," Iris said, her voice pleading. "But it's the truth. And now that you know, you're in more danger than ever."

Mallory stared at her mother. "You kept quiet all these years. Why now? Why tell me now?"

Maggie stepped in. "Because you read the journals. You've already started piecing it together. And whether you believe it or not, there are others who will figure it out, too. If they find out who you are..."

Mallory's breath caught. "I need time to think," she said, her voice steady despite the storm inside her.

THE NIGHT WAS COLD and unforgiving by the time Mallory made the drive across town to Garret's house. As she pulled up to the modest two-story house, she noticed the warm glow of light spilling from the windows, a stark contrast to the bitter darkness outside. Her hands trembled as she cut the engine and stepped out into the icy air, her breath puffing out in small clouds.

The faint hum of voices and Boone's sharp bark greeted her as she climbed the porch steps. A moment later, Garret appeared, pushing the screen door open. His brows furrowed when he saw her face, pale and tight with unspoken thoughts.

"Hey," he said softly. "You okay?"

Mallory nodded, though the gesture felt hollow. "Yeah, but I need to talk to y'all about something. It's important."

The warmth of the house wrapped around her, carrying the comforting scent of wood smoke and pepperoni pizza. Boone bounded over, his tail wagging furiously as he nuzzled her leg. She crouched down to scratch behind his ears, grateful for the brief moment of normalcy.

"They're in the living room," Garret said, gesturing toward the open doorway.

Inside, Ryan and Josie were seated around the coffee table, which was covered with a chaotic spread of case files, old letters, and half-eaten slices of pizza. Josie glanced up first, her sharp eyes immediately zeroing in on Mallory's tense expression. Ryan followed, his face lighting up with a welcoming smile that quickly faded as he noticed her unease.

"Mallory," Josie said, setting down a folder. "What's going on?"

Mallory hesitated and sank onto the couch next to Garret, her fingers twisting together in her lap. Boone sat at her feet, leaning against her leg as if sensing her distress. "I just came from my mom's house," she began, her voice low but steady. "And Maggie Whitaker was there. They uh... they told me some things that I think you all need to hear."

Garret leaned forward, his elbows resting on his knees. "What kind of things?"

Mallory took a deep breath. "I'm a descendant of Susannah Fairchild and Tobias Bennington. Their daughter, Hope, was my great-grandmother."

Ryan's brows shot up. "Wait, are you serious?"

"Dead serious," Mallory replied. "But that's not the worst part. My mom and Maggie, they've known about the cult stuff their whole lives. They say that some people in this town, people like Reverend Bennington, still believe there's something special about our bloodline. Maggie and Mama say it's something dangerous."

Josie's eyes narrowed. "Dangerous how?"

"I'm not sure if they even know. They didn't give me details," Mallory admitted. "But from what I've read in Susannah's journal and what they said tonight, it sounds like they believe in sacrificial rituals. Silas Bennington thought he could gain power through them. Anyway, I don't know who all is in this cult, but it's been around since the 1800s. And now, whoever's in charge… well, I think they're trying to perform the same kind of rituals Bennington did back then. *That's* why the girls went missing."

Garret's jaw tightened. "So, they wanted to use the missing women in a ritual—a *sacrificial* ritual?"

"Does that mean they're dead?"

Mallory sighed. "I don't know if they're dead yet. But Lila, Sadie, Claire, and Natalie… What if they're not random victims? What if they all have Bennington blood in their family lines somewhere? That would explain why they were targeted."

Josie's fingers tapped against the edge of the table, her mind clearly racing. "All of them being descendants of Bennington? I don't know. It kinda sounds like a long shot, but it's worth looking into."

Ryan flipped open a notebook, jotting something down. "We'll need to dig into their family histories."

"That'll take time," Garret said, "but it's not impossible. We can start with genealogy records, maybe cross-reference with the journals."

"And we'll need to be discreet," Josie added. "We don't know who's in this cult. It could be anyone. And, if someone's targeting women with Bennington blood, we don't want to tip them off that we're onto them."

Mallory swallowed hard. "I'll help with the research. Whatever it takes to figure this out."

THE MOONLIGHT SPILLED through the windows of Garret's living room, illuminating the cluttered table that now served as their makeshift research hub. Stacks of genealogy records, old photographs, and handwritten notes were spread out in organized chaos. Mallory sat cross-legged on the floor, her laptop balanced on her knees, while Josie thumbed through a thick binder of local archives. Garret and Ryan hovered over a map of Blackwater Ridge, marking key locations with red pins.

"Okay," Mallory said, breaking the silence, "I've traced Lila Dawson's family tree back to the late 1800s. Her great-great-grandfather was Corbin Bennington's son, Joseph. He moved out west after Silas' death, but the bloodline stayed intact."

"That's one connection," Garret said, nodding as he marked Lila's name on a notepad. "What about the others?"

"Sadie Harper's family is a little trickier," Josie chimed in, flipping a page in the binder. "Her great-grandmother was Corbin's daughter, which makes her a direct descendant as well. Same bloodline, just another branch."

Ryan leaned back in his chair, tapping a pencil against the table. "So far, it's all coming back to Corbin. What about Natalie Baxter?"

Mallory typed furiously on her keyboard, her brow furrowing in concentration. "Give me a second. I found a census record that might help." After a few moments, she let out a triumphant "Aha," and spun the laptop around for the others to see. "Natalie's great-great-grandmother was also one of Corbin's descendants. Her branch of the family settled near Blackwater Ridge for a while before spreading out."

"So, all three of them—Lila, Sadie, and Natalie—are from Corbin's line," Garret concluded, leaning over the table. "Does Claire Crawford fit that pattern?"

"No, she doesn't," Mallory said, her voice thoughtful. "Which makes her the outlier. We need to dig deeper into her family tree."

The room fell silent as they focused on their tasks. Josie frowned as she pored over old records. "I thought Claire had no ties to Blackwater Ridge," she said. "But there's something odd here."

"What is it?" Mallory asked, leaning closer.

"Her grandmother, Rose Crawford, was born Rose Bennington," Josie said, her voice tinged with surprise. "She was Silas' illegitimate daughter—Katherine's child. It looks like she changed her name after moving to the city."

Ryan's eyes widened. "An illegitimate child? That's new information. Did Silas acknowledge her?"

"Not officially," Josie said. "But there are enough documents linking her to him. It looks like Katherine's descendants stayed in the area for a while before scattering."

Mallory's eyes widened. "So Claire's not from Corbin's line at all. She descended from Silas' secret daughter."

Garret's jaw tightened. "How did we miss this?"

"We didn't know to look for it," Mallory said. "But get this—Claire's family inherited some property on the outskirts of town. It used to belong to Silas."

Josie's face darkened. "I don't think I like where this is going."

Mallory's fingers hovered over the keyboard, her mind racing. "If Claire knew about her connection to the Benningtons, she might've known about the rituals, too. What if she's not a victim?"

Garret stood up, pacing the length of the living room. "We need to find out everything we can about Claire—where she's been, who she's been talking to, anything that connects her to the missing women."

"And we need to move fast," Josie added. "If Claire's involved, she could be dangerous."

Mallory nodded, determination hardening her features. "We'll start with her family's property. If there's anything there that ties her to what's happening, we'll find it."

"Only one problem." Garret said causing the other three to look up at him. "We need a warrant to search that property, and we can't get one here in Blackwater Ridge without tipping people off."

Boone let out a low growl from his spot by the couch. Mallory glanced down at him, then back at her friends. "Whatever Claire's hiding, we're going to uncover it. And if she's part of this, we'll stop her." She looked back up at Garret, "I'll handle the warrant. She's technically still a victim so I don't think I'll have any problems with that."

Chapter Seventeen

Mallory tossed and turned, visions of a young girl fighting for her life dancing through her dreams. She woke with a start and sighed before glancing at the clock beside the bed.

"Ugh, it's only four in the morning?" she whined before throwing the covers back and flipping on the light as she stomped to the small coffee pot on the counter in her room. She made the coffee, and once it had finished brewing, she poured the steaming liquid into a mug. As she put the mug to her lips, she saw her bag sitting on the table across the room.

She padded softly over to the table and sat down, pulling the bag into her lap. She slowly pulled out two worn leather journals from the bag and studied them for a moment. She closed her eyes before opening the one that belonged to Silas Bennington.

April 25, 1894

That wretched girl! It must have been she who aided the other in making her escape under the cover of darkness. For days, my men have scoured the woods surrounding the cave, yet no trace of them has been found. Susannah was nigh upon her time of delivery, and thus I know they could not have ventured far. Yet, where are they?

Though the vile girls and the child may have eluded my grasp for the present, they shall not run forever. The blood of my forebears courses through the veins of that child and Esther alike. They are mine, by right and by blood. And through this innocent babe, I shall ensure that the darkness endures. Should it require many generations, the mountain will reclaim what is rightfully owed.

She closed the journal, tears streaking down her face. "Silas knew he couldn't stop them, but he thought the darkness would live on through his bloodline. Through *me*," she whispered to herself in the quiet room.

Mallory continued to sit at the table long after she had closed the journal. Silas' words weighed down on her spirit. Taking a deep breath, she wiped her tears and decided that focusing on the task ahead was better than sitting there crying. The missing women needed her to find them—there was no time for self-pity.

At 6 A.M., Mallory walked into Garret's living room, their unofficial headquarters. Boone raised his head from his spot by the couch, his tail thumping lazily against the floor in greeting. The others were already there. Josie and Ryan sat side by side at the cluttered table, sifting through a growing stack of documents. Garret stood by the counter, holding four steaming cups of coffee. He looked up as Mallory entered, his face weary but alert.

"Good morning, Mallory," Garret said, offering her a cup. "I take it you couldn't sleep either?"

She shook her head, taking the coffee with a small smile. "Dreams kept me awake. Dreams of a young girl fighting for her life. It's like my subconscious is trying to piece a puzzle together."

Josie glanced up. "You okay? You look like you've been up for a while."

"I am," Mallory said, setting the coffee down and pulling out Silas's journal. "I've been going through this again. There's something we've missed, something important."

Ryan leaned back in his chair, frowning. "We've been through those journals a dozen times. What could we have missed?"

Mallory opened the journal to the passage she had read earlier. Her voice was steady, but a faint tremor betrayed her unease as she read aloud Silas' words about the darkness living on through his bloodline. When she finished, the room was silent.

Finally, Garret said, "If Silas believed the darkness could survive through his descendants, and this group believes the same thing, then Claire's involvement isn't a coincidence. She *has* to be a part of their plan."

"Unfortunately, that plan likely involves *all* of the missing women," Mallory said, her gaze flickering to Esther's journal lying open on the table. "But why? We've been so focused on finding them that we haven't even considered *why* they're being taken."

Josie crossed her arms, leaning against the edge of the table. "If they're targeting descendants of Corbin, maybe the women stumbled onto something they weren't supposed to."

Mallory's fingers brushed against the locket around her neck, and she paused. A sudden chill ran through her. She opened the locket, and her eyes widened as the memory of an entry from Susannah's journal came to her mind.

"Garret," she said, her voice trembling with realization. "This locket belonged to Hope. It's the same one Susannah mentioned in her journal. The key inside isn't just symbolic—it's real."

Garret leaned forward, his expression a mixture of urgency and shock. "If that key unlocks something tied to Bennington's legacy, it could be the break we've been waiting for. Do you have any idea where the chest might be?"

Mallory nodded slowly. "There's a passage in Esther's journal. She wrote about a small cave near the river where they sought refuge after Susannah died. She described it as a place hidden and so out of reach that even Silas couldn't find it. That could be where she hid the chest."

Ryan whistled softly. "A hidden cave near the river? That's a lot of ground to cover."

"Yeah, but we've got to try," Garret said, grabbing his coat. "If this key leads us to answers, we can't waste any more time."

AS THEY APPROACHED the riverbank, they heard rushing water flowing through the mountain. Boone trotted ahead, his nose searching the ground. They had parked the SUV a mile away, choosing to hike the rest of the way to avoid drawing attention in case someone was in the area.

"There," Mallory called, pointing to a cluster of rocks partially hidden by overgrown foliage. The cave entrance was small, barely noticeable unless someone knew it was there and was searching for it.

They approached the entrance cautiously, their flashlights illuminating the narrow path that led into the cave. Josie and Ryan flanked Mallory and Garret, their weapons ready. The air grew colder as they followed the steep path deeper inside, where the walls were damp and covered with moss. After a couple of minutes, they reached a small recess where the ground leveled out.

"It doesn't look like anyone's been in here in a long time," Mallory said, scanning the area.

Garret nodded. "Which might be a good thing if that chest is here somewhere. It probably means Silas and his followers never found it."

Josie glanced around the cave, her flashlight beam darting over the walls. "This place gives me the creeps, but it's definitely the kind of spot someone would use to hide something important."

Ryan stepped closer to the others. "Let's just hope we're the first ones to find it."

Something flashed in the beam of Mallory's flashlight as she searched the ground. Her heart pounded as she moved toward the spot. "Garret, I think this might be it," she called, kneeling in the corner of the cave. She quickly moved some debris from the wooden crate in front of her. She brushed away the dirt that had caked onto the chest over years of abandonment, revealing intricate carvings on its surface.

She pulled the locket from her neck, removed the key, and inserted it into the lock. She turned the key gently, and the lock clicked open.

The chest creaked loudly as it opened, its hinges rusty from years of neglect. Inside, its contents were revealed: a collection of faded letters that were remarkably still legible and a small satchel filled with what appeared to be dried herbs.

Garret picked up the letters gently. "The letters are addressed to Hope." He handed one to Mallory.

She unfolded the fragile, yellowed paper, her eyes scanning the dainty handwriting. "This one mentions a man named Amos Jameson," she said. "Susannah warns Hope to stay away from him, calling him a 'loyal servant of Silas and the darkness that consumes him.'"

Garret's expression darkened. "Amos Jameson? How can that be? He's the owner of the lodge over by the ridge—the one we've been keeping tabs on since Natalie went missing. But that doesn't make any sense. It can't be the same person. He'd have to be well over a hundred years old by now."

Mallory shook her head. "It's likely that the Amos from the late 1800s is an ancestor of *our* Amos. I bet he knows something, though. I'd say he's our next lead, so we need to have another conversation with him immediately."

Josie exchanged a look with Ryan, her voice tense. "If he's involved, he might already know we're onto him. We should be careful."

By the time they reached the lodge, the early afternoon sun was high in the sky, casting dark shadows that appeared to dance over the property. Mallory's stomach dropped as they approached the front door, the weight of the locket pressing tightly against her chest.

Amos Jameson greeted them with a tight but polite smile, his weathered face showing no hint of distress. "Sheriff Cole, Agent Crane. To what do I owe the pleasure of this visit?"

"We need to ask you a few questions," Garret said, his tone firm but calculated. "About some things that have happened in the area recently."

Amos waved them in. "Of course. I told you I would help in any way I could. Please come in. Make yourselves comfortable."

The lodge's interior was cozy, with antique furniture displayed proudly and the faint scent of wood smoke lingering in the air. Amos led them to a sitting area near the fireplace, where he poured several cups of coffee. Josie and Ryan stood nearby, their expressions tense.

"So," Amos said, glancing at them before taking a seat. "What's this visit about? Not another missing girl, I hope."

Mallory wasted no time getting to the point of their visit. "Amos, we have reason to believe that you may be connected to the group responsible for the disappearances. Specifically, we'd like to know about any relationship you may have with Silas Bennington's descendants."

For the smallest moment, Amos' eyes flickered with something—recognition, perhaps—but his expression remained steady and undisturbed. "I'm sorry, what are you talking about?"

"Don't play coy, Mr. Jameson," Garret said, his voice low. "We've got letters that link your family to the Bennington family. And we believe you're still just as connected as your great-grandfather was."

Amos' smile faltered slightly. He leaned back in his chair, crossing his arms, his gaze steady. "Now you're digging into things you simply don't understand. Silas' work is far from over, and none of you have what it takes to stop it."

Mallory's hand instinctively moved to her holster. "You need to tell us where the women are," she demanded.

Amos laughed darkly. "Even if I tell you where they are, you won't make it in time. The wheels have already been set in motion."

Before they could react, Amos jumped from his chair, knocking over the coffee table as he sprinted toward a side door. Garret and Ryan gave chase. Mallory followed, her gun drawn and ready. Boone, alerted by the commotion, tore past her, his sharp bark echoing through the woods behind the lodge.

Garret was just steps behind Amos, his hand outstretched. He was nearly able to grab the man's coat when Amos suddenly twisted left, darting off the trail and disappearing into the thick underbrush. Garret hesitated for a moment, catching sight of Ryan close behind him before diving into the foliage after Amos.

Josie emerged from the lodge just as Mallory reached the trail's edge. "He went this way," Mallory said, motioning for Josie to follow.

The dense trees cast shifting shadows, and the sound of branches snapping grew faint. Boone, by Mallory's side, growled low and sniffed the ground.

"Garret!" Mallory shouted. "Do you see him, boy?"

A muffled reply came from deeper in the woods. "He's heading uphill! Stay on the trail—we'll corner him up ahead!"

Mallory hesitated, her instincts torn. Something about Amos' arrogance concerned her. Her gut told her he knew something they didn't. Her mind raced with possibilities as she took off down the path, Josie close behind her, both scanning every direction for any sign of movement.

As they rounded a bend in the path, the sound of a struggle reached them. Garret's voice raised in a shout, followed by the sound of a body hitting the ground. Boone rushed ahead, and Mallory and Josie followed.

They found Garret struggling with Amos near a rocky ledge. Amos twisted and fought with surprising strength for a man his age, his face filled with anger.

In his right hand, his grip was tight around what looked like an antique dagger, its blade glinting eerily in the fading light.

"Drop it, Amos," Mallory demanded, aiming her weapon at him.

Amos froze, his eyes locking onto hers. His eyes seemed almost completely black. Then, for a moment, the woods seemed to hold its breath.

"You don't understand. You *can't* understand," Amos growled, his voice low and full of venom. "You're meddling in things far older and stronger than you are. This isn't just about Silas or his legacy. This is about survival—yours and everyone else's."

"Drop the weapon. I won't tell you again," Mallory repeated, her voice steady despite the anger and fear coursing through her.

Amos glanced between her, Garret, and Josie before a twisted laugh escaped his lips. "You're too late," he whispered.

In a blur of chaotic motion, he slashed the dagger into his own palm, and blood dripped onto the forest floor. The ground beneath them rumbled.

"What the hell was that?" Garret muttered.

Mallory stepped closer, her eyes darting between Amos and the strange marks carved into the dagger. "What did you just do, Amos?"

He let out a wheezing laugh. "I just opened a door. You think you're ready? Let's see if you can handle what comes through."

The rumbling stopped as quickly as it had begun, leaving an eerie silence in its wake. Mallory exchanged a look with Garret, her stomach knotting with unease.

"Grab him," she ordered, her voice sharper than she intended. "We need answers, and he's going to give them to us right now."

Garret reached for Amos, but the older man was too quick, even injured. With an evil laugh, Amos moved closer to the ledge.

"You'll never be able to stop it now. This is the end. You've already lost," he said before throwing himself into the deep valley below.

"No!" Mallory yelled, rushing toward the ledge.

Josie knelt beside her, scanning the valley below with wide eyes.

"What the hell just happened?" Mallory asked breathlessly, turning to Garret.

Garret stood shaken. "I have no idea. He was right there. How did I miss him when I grabbed for him? I just... I just don't know."

"We need to figure out how to get down into that valley to search for his body," Mallory said. "Let's head back to the lodge."

The short hike back to the lodge was heavy with unspoken tension, the quiet broken only by the crunch of boots on fallen leaves and the occasional rustle of wind through the trees. The forest, normally alive with sound, seemed eerily subdued, as if nature itself was holding its breath.

Garret's face was drawn, his jaw clenched tightly as he led the way. Josie trailed slightly behind, her eyes scanning their surroundings as if expecting the shadows to shift into something unnatural. Ryan stayed close to Mallory, his hand resting on the butt of his gun. Boone padded alongside them, his ears flicking in every direction.

As the lodge came into view through the thinning trees, its rustic charm seemed to take on a darker tone, the cheerful façade now overshadowed by the sinister events unfolding. The back entrance loomed ahead, a stark reminder of the secrets the building might hold.

Garret finally broke the silence as they reached the door. "I need to call this in. We need a search team to go down into that valley and recover his body." His eyes flicked toward the distant ridge as if Amos might somehow reappear.

Mallory nodded, her face set with determination. "We also need to search this place top to bottom for evidence. There's no way he didn't leave something behind. I'll call Larkin and see if I can get a rush on a warrant. Under the circumstances, I don't think it'll be an issue."

Without waiting for a reply, Mallory stepped to the side, pulling out her phone as she walked a few paces away.

Behind her, Garret pulled out his radio and contacted dispatch.

The phone rang twice. "This is Larkin," he answered.

Mallory took a steadying breath, stepping farther from the others to avoid distraction. "Hey, it's Mallory. I need a favor," she said.

There was a brief silence before Larkin replied. "What do you need?"

Her words tumbled out quickly, each one laden with urgency. "Amos Jameson, owner of the Ridgeview Lodge, just threw himself off the ridge. We have strong reason to believe he's connected to the abduction of our missing women. I need a warrant to search the lodge, and I need it now. This is time-sensitive."

On the other end of the line, Larkin groaned. "Shit. What the hell is going on down there?"

Mallory rubbed her temple, glancing back toward the lodge. Its darkened windows seemed to stare back at her, indifferent and impenetrable. "I'm honestly not sure, sir," she admitted. "But whatever it is, it's bigger than we expected. Amos said things... things that don't add up. And then he..." She trailed off, the image of Amos' unsettling smile and his cryptic words flashing in her mind.

Larkin sighed deeply, the sound of papers rustling in the background. "Alright, Crane. I'll pull some strings and get you that warrant. It'll take a few hours at most. You stay put until then. Don't go in until you have that warrant in hand. Understood?"

"Yes, sir," Mallory replied.

As she ended the call, the crunch of approaching footsteps pulled her attention. Garret stood a few feet away, his face etched with concern. "Larkin's getting us the warrant?"

She nodded. "Yeah, but it'll take a few hours. He doesn't want us going in until we have it."

Garret frowned, glancing toward the lodge. "Fine with me. That place gives me the creeps. Feels like it's watching us."

"Trust me. You're not the only one feeling that," Mallory muttered.

Josie and Ryan joined them, "What's the plan until then?" Josie asked.

Mallory squared her shoulders. "We wait, but we stay alert. Amos might be gone, but I don't trust that we've seen the last of whatever he was involved in."

Ryan gestured toward the lodge. "Should we secure the perimeter? Make sure no one else is lurking around?"

Mallory hesitated, then nodded. "Good idea. Josie, Ryan, you two take the north and east sides. Garret and I will cover the south and west. Keep your radios on, and call in if you see anything—*anything*—out of place."

As they moved to their positions, the lodge seemed to loom even larger in the fading light, its shadow stretching across the ground like an ominous warning. Mallory's hand hovered near her holster. Boone stayed close to her side, his ears perked and his nose twitching as he sniffed the air.

The minutes dragged into an hour, and just as Mallory was about to radio the others, Boone let out a low growl.

"What is it, boy?" she whispered, following his gaze.

In the distance, barely visible through the dense trees, a flicker of movement caught her eye.

Something—or someone—was watching them.

Chapter Eighteen

Two hours later, Mallory's phone buzzed with a text from Agent Larkin, confirming that the warrant to search the lodge had been secured. She glanced at the message before quickly picking up her radio. "Hey guys, meet me at the front entrance. The warrant just came through," she called out.

At the front entrance, Garret stood, his face serious as he briefed her. "I confirmed with the night clerk that there's only one guest on site, and I spoke to the guest directly. He's just passing through on his way to his daughter's wedding in Savannah. I cleared him quickly and arranged for him to head over to the Blackwater Ridge Inn."

Ryan, scanning the area, furrowed his brow. "Alright, so how are we handling this?"

Garret glanced at Mallory, giving her a brief nod. She met his eyes and then addressed the group with a sharp, authoritative tone. "Josie, you and Garret take the first floor and the basement. Ryan and I will handle the second floor and the attic. Let's move quickly and stay in contact."

"Got it," came the chorus of affirmations from the team.

Mallory led Ryan and Boone toward the staircase, the ancient wooden boards creaking beneath their weight. The air grew colder as they ascended, the faint scent of mildew mingling with something metallic. The second floor was dimly lit, the windows cloaked in heavy curtains.

"This place is weird. Why in the hell would anyone want to stay here?" Ryan asked as they searched the guest rooms.

Mallory nodded, her pulse quickening. She gestured for Boone to stay close and stepped cautiously toward the door. The old wood groaned as she pushed it open, revealing a room that was startlingly different from the rest of the lodge.

Unlike the other rooms, this one was meticulously clean. A desk sat against the far wall, its surface covered with neatly arranged papers and an open laptop. A large corkboard hung on one side, pinned with photographs, maps, and strings connecting various points. A small bookshelf held an assortment of leather-bound journals, their spines cracked with age.

"Ryan, check the desk," Mallory instructed, moving toward the corkboard. Boone sniffed the air, his attention drawn to a corner of the room where a trunk sat partially hidden beneath a tarp.

Mallory's eyes scanned the board, her stomach sinking as she recognized some of the faces in the photographs. Missing women. Each photo was marked with handwritten notes—dates, locations, and cryptic symbols she didn't recognize. Her gaze settled on one photo near the center of the board: Claire. Unlike the others, her picture had no notes, only a red circle drawn around it.

"Mallory, you're gonna want to see this," Ryan called from the desk.

She turned, crossing the room to join him. He pointed to a stack of documents—ledger pages listing names, dates, and amounts of money. Beside them, a small notebook lay open, its pages filled with entries detailing transactions and activities that sent a chill down her spine.

"It's a ledger," Ryan said. "Looks like payments were made to keep certain things quiet. There's a lot of money changing hands here, and some of these names are familiar."

Mallory scanned the pages, her fingers brushing against the notebook. "These notes... they're talking about the women. Times and places they were taken, who was involved. This is a paper trail tying Amos directly to the disappearances."

"And it gets worse," Ryan added, holding up a photograph he'd found beneath the papers. It was a picture of Claire, standing beside Amos. Her expression was tense, her eyes filled with a mix of fear and what looked like amusement.

Mallory's jaw tightened. "This ties Claire to him. Whether she's a victim or involved, we need to find out."

Boone barked sharply, drawing their attention. He pawed at the trunk in the corner, whining. Mallory moved quickly, kneeling beside him as she carefully pulled the tarp away. The trunk was old, its metal latches rusted but intact. She opened it cautiously, her breath catching, at the sight inside.

The trunk was filled with items that seemed both mundane and deeply personal. Jewelry, small trinkets, and scraps of clothing lay atop a stack of bound journals. Beneath them, a bundle of letters tied with a ribbon caught her eye. She pulled them out, her hands trembling as she read the first one.

The letter was addressed to Amos, written in a flowing script that spoke of desperation and fear. The writer begged him to release someone named "Anna," warning of dire consequences if he didn't. The dates on the letters spanned decades, some as recent as a year ago.

"These are trophies," Mallory said softly, her voice barely above a whisper. "And these journals..." She opened one, her stomach churning at the detailed accounts of rituals, sacrifices, and cryptic references to "Silas' work."

Ryan looked over her shoulder, his face pale. "This is insane. He's been keeping records of everything."

Mallory nodded, her mind racing. "This is enough to bring down more than just Amos. These journals could expose an entire network. But we need to focus on Claire. If she's connected to this, she might be in danger... or worse."

Her radio crackled to life, Garret's voice cutting through. "We found a hidden room in the basement. You two need to see this."

Mallory exchanged a grim look with Ryan, tucking the letters and one of the journals into an evidence bag. "Let's go," she said, leading the way downstairs.

The basement was cold and damp, the faint smell of decay hanging in the air. Garret and Josie stood near a section of the wall that had been pulled away to reveal a hidden passage. The opening led to a small, windowless room lit by a single, flickering bulb.

Mallory stepped inside, her breath hitching as she took in the sight before her. The walls were lined with shelves holding jars filled with strange, murky substances. A table in the center of the room was covered with ritualistic tools—candles, a ceremonial dagger, and a large tome opened to a page depicting a symbol she'd seen on the corkboard upstairs.

"It's a ritual room," Josie said quietly, her voice trembling. "He was performing ceremonies down here."

Garret pointed to a set of chains bolted to the far wall, their ends stained with what looked like dried blood. "It looks like he was holding people here."

Mallory moved closer, her flashlight tracing the path of the chains. Beside the chains, scratch marks gouged into the stone wall suggested someone had fought desperately against their restraints. She crouched down, running her fingers just above the surface of the markings, her chest tightening with each jagged line.

Josie's voice broke the tense silence. "Look at this." She stood near a corner of the room, holding up a tattered piece of fabric. It was stained and torn, but Mallory recognized the distinct pattern immediately—a floral print that matched the blouse Claire had been wearing in her last-known photograph.

Mallory's stomach dropped. "That's Claire's," she murmured, taking the fabric from Josie.

Ryan's voice came from across the room, low and grim. "There's more." He stood near an overturned crate, its contents spilled haphazardly onto the floor. Among the debris were personal items—a silver locket, a cracked phone case, and a woman's scarf. "These must belong to the others," Ryan said.

Mallory nodded, her throat tight. "He was definitely keeping trophies."

Garret knelt beside the crate, carefully sifting through the items. "If we catalog these, we might be able to connect them to other missing women. This is solid evidence."

"Look at this," Josie said again, her voice sharper this time. She had moved to a crude wooden desk on the other side of the room. On its surface lay an open ledger, its pages filled with meticulous notes. Beside the ledger was an old map, its edges frayed and yellowed with age. Several locations were marked with red Xs, each one accompanied by a date.

Mallory moved to Josie's side, scanning the map. Her breath caught when she saw that one of the Xs was labeled with the date from Claire's notebook—tomorrow.

"Garret," Mallory said, her voice urgent. "Look at this."

He joined her, his brow furrowing as he studied the map. "These locations... they're spread out, but they all center around this area." He pointed to a remote stretch of forest about two miles north of the lodge.

Ryan frowned. "Where is that?"

"About half a mile from the church," Garret replied.

Mallory's gaze shifted to the ledger. The notes were written in a strange mix of cryptic symbols and plain English, but one entry stood out: *The Offering—final preparation complete. Tomorrow.*' Her pulse quickened as she read the words.

"We need to move now," she said, her voice firm. "This isn't just evidence of what he's done—it's a roadmap for what he's planning. Claire's life depends on us getting to that location before he does."

Garret nodded, already pulling out his radio to call in additional units. "We'll need a full team, equipped for a wilderness search. And someone to start decoding that ledger—it might tell us more about what we're walking into."

Josie and Ryan exchanged a tense glance but didn't hesitate. Ryan moved to gather the evidence, while Josie snapped photos of the room and its contents for documentation.

As they worked, Mallory's thoughts raced. She couldn't shake the feeling that they were running out of time.

Finally, Garret's voice cut through the room. "Backup's on its way. Let's pack this up and get moving. We've got a lead, and we're not letting it slip through our fingers."

Mallory gave a sharp nod. "Let's find them."

AS THE DARK, WINDING road stretched ahead, the only sounds in the SUV were the hum of the engine and the occasional rattle of gravel beneath the tires. Mallory sat in the passenger seat, scanning the trees that lined the road leading to the area marked on the map.

Suddenly, the silence was broken by the sharp buzz of her phone vibrating in the cup holder. Mallory's pulse quickened when she saw Caleb Maynard's name on the screen. She grabbed the phone, her hands trembling as she answered.

"Agent Crane," Caleb's voice came through. "I... I'm sorry to bother you this late, but there's something, um... something strange happening out here. I think it might be connected to your case."

Mallory's stomach dropped. She motioned for Garret to pull over, her eyes locked on the dark stretch of road ahead as she spoke. "What do you mean?"

"It's on the back half of my property, near where the old mill used to stand. There's been movement in the woods. I saw lights—flashlights, I think. And vehicles driving up through the property off the old access road. And just now, I heard…" Caleb hesitated. "Chanting. A low, rhythmic chanting. It's not… normal."

Garret's grip on the steering wheel tightened, and Ryan leaned in from the back seat, listening intently. Mallory's mind raced. "Did you see anyone? Did anyone see you? Did you see the vehicles or just hear them?"

"Other than the light from the flashlights and headlights from what looked like a truck or van, I didn't see anything else. It's dark out here, hard to make out much past my hand," Caleb replied. "But I did hear voices. As they moved toward the mill, a woman's voice stood out. She sounded like she was in charge."

Mallory felt a cold knot form in her stomach. "Alright, Caleb. We're on our way. Stay inside, lock your doors, and don't open them until Garret, Deputy Taylor, or I come to get you." She ended the call, her fingers tightening around the phone before she turned to Garret, her voice steady but filled with strength. "This could be it."

Garret nodded, already signaling for the turnaround. "Let's hope we can put an end to this once and for all. Tonight."

The drive to Caleb's property seemed to stretch on forever. When they finally arrived, the air was thick with the smell of wood burning, mixed with something metallic and pungent—blood, perhaps?

They quickly made their way onto the porch, and Caleb opened the door, his face pale as he gripped a shotgun tightly in his right hand. His eyes flickered nervously toward the tree line.

"It's coming from over there," Caleb said in a hushed voice, pointing toward the thicket of trees behind the house. "Whatever they're doing, it's not good. I can feel it in my bones."

Mallory placed a reassuring hand on his shoulder. "Stay here, Caleb. Keep the doors locked no matter what you hear or see. We'll handle it from here."

Just as they were about to step off the porch, Mallory's team arrived in full force. Mallory gave them a grim nod, and they quickly gathered around the SUV to go over their plan.

Garret, ever the tactician, pulled his flashlight from his belt. "Alright, we need to be smart about this. There are seven of us, but we don't know how many of them we're up against. Keep your weapons drawn, and stay alert."

Mallory glanced at her team. Josie's face was set in determination, her hand resting lightly on her weapon as she glanced toward the shadows of the trees.

"Our main objective is to stop whatever ritual they're performing and get the missing women to safety. Second, we need to arrest anyone responsible for this," Garret continued.

Mallory nodded. "We know what we need to do. Stay safe, and let's move out."

Boone trotted alongside Garrett, his ears perked up and his nose sniffing the air. Together, they led the group toward the back of the house, where the dark woods beckoned.

As they neared the old mill, Mallory's heart rate sped up. She could just make out the glow of lanterns through the trees and the flickering light of what seemed to be a fire in the center of a clearing.

They halted just before the clearing, crouching behind a thick cluster of bushes. From this vantage point, they saw the group gathered in a circle around a large stone altar. The symbols carved into its surface matched the ones Mallory had seen before—the markings in the church and on the walls of the cave where Susannah had been held hostage.

In the center of the circle, Claire Crawford stood tall, her long black cloak billowing in the wind, her wild hair cascading around her shoulders. The flickering firelight cast an eerie glow across her face as she chanted in a language Mallory had never heard before.

Beside Claire, Darla Hensley knelt, holding a large, open book in her hands. Around them stood several other figures, their heads bowed in silent reverence. Mallory's gaze shifted, and her breath caught as she saw the two women sitting bound and gagged near the altar. It was Lila and Natalie.

Garret whispered, "Look, there are the other two missing women. They're alive."

Mallory's grip on her weapon tightened. "Yeah, and it looks like our guts were right about Claire being involved. We need to act fast. We can't let them finish that ritual."

With a silent signal, Garret crept around to the opposite side of the clearing, taking up a concealed position. Boone stayed at Mallory's side, watching intently. Mallory took a deep breath, her eyes never leaving Claire. She stepped out of the shadows, her voice cutting through the night air like a blade.

"FBI! Drop the book, Darla, and step away from the altar!"

The chanting ceased abruptly, and Claire slowly turned, her face unsettlingly calm. She looked directly at Mallory, her eyes dark with malice.

"You're too late, Agent Crane," Claire said, her voice calm but laced with a hint of mockery. "Or should I say... cousin? Yes, Mallory, I know about your Bennington bloodline. But even you can't stop the Darkness. It's already here."

Mallory's stomach twisted, but she held her ground, refusing to show weakness. "You're right. I *am* part of the Bennington bloodline. But unlike you, I don't follow the batshit crazy principles of Silas Bennington." She stepped forward, her gun trained directly on Claire. "Release the women and put your hands in the air. Now."

Claire's lips curled into a cold, humorless smile. "You think you can stop me? I don't think so. You might have won this battle, but I will win the war. And you, my friend, have a huge role to play."

Before Mallory could respond, Darla leapt to her feet, clutching a vial of crimson liquid in her hand. "Claire, it's done! The seal has been broken!"

"Not if I have anything to say about it," Garret shouted, emerging from cover. He fired a warning shot into the air, and the group of cult members scrambled in every direction. Boone was the first to react, charging into the clearing, growling and snapping at their heels.

Ryan, Josie, and the rest of the team followed quickly, forcing the fleeing figures to the ground and restraining them. Mallory dashed toward Claire, but the woman moved with unnatural speed, disappearing into the trees before Mallory could catch her.

Darla dropped the book and the vial of blood, trying to flee, but Boone was on her in an instant, knocking her to the ground.

"Garret, the women," Mallory shouted as she cuffed Darla, her eyes sweeping the clearing for Lila and Natalie.

Garret was already kneeling beside the two women, cutting the zip ties around their wrists and ankles. "You're safe now," he said.

Suddenly, the ground beneath them trembled, and the altar glowed with a faint, red light. Mallory's eyes widened in alarm. "We need to destroy the altar, now," she shouted.

Ryan rushed forward, grabbing a heavy branch. Together, they slammed it against the stone altar, cracking it with a resounding thud. The red glow dissipated, and the tremors stopped.

"It's not over yet," Mallory said, her breath coming in sharp gasps as she took in the scene. "Claire got away, and whatever she started, she'll try to finish. But at least we have Darla and the others."

Garret nodded, gently guiding the freed women toward the safety of Caleb's house. Boone stayed close, vigilant as always. Mallory cast one last glance at the shattered altar, her resolve hardening.

The battle was far from over.

Chapter Nineteen

The small interrogation room at the sheriff's station was suffocatingly silent, save for the faint hum of the flickering fluorescent light overhead. Its weak, stuttering glow cast harsh shadows along the cracked walls, further deepening the oppressive atmosphere. Darla sat slumped in a metal chair, her wrists cuffed tightly to the table in front of her, her attorney at her side. She looked disheveled—her face pale, eyes bloodshot, a mix of defiance and exhaustion etched into every feature. Her once-pristine black clothing now hung loosely around her frail frame.

Across from her sat Mallory and Garret. In the corner, FBI Agent Logan Archer stood, his sharp gaze trained on Darla as he quietly observed, his laptop open, recording every word for posterity. Mallory's fingers drummed lightly on the edge of the table.

Finally, she leaned forward. "Darla, we have you dead to rights. Attempted murder, conspiracy, kidnapping. And not to mention aiding and abetting Claire in whatever sick ritual she was trying to complete. If you cooperate, it could help your case."

Darla's lips twitched. She shook her head slowly, her voice laced with disdain. "You just don't get it, do you?" Her attorney tried to quiet her, but she kept going. "This is bigger than you. Bigger than me. The Bennington bloodline—it's destiny. You're all just pawns in something far older than you could ever understand."

"Destiny?" Garret snapped. His knuckles whitened as his hands clenched into fists. "Spare us the sermon, Darla. What was Claire trying to do tonight? What was her goal?"

For a moment, Darla's eyes flicked nervously between them, as if weighing the risk of saying too much. She hesitated, but after a long moment, her shoulders slumped, a tired sigh escaping her lips. "Fine. You really want to know? The rituals—the sacrifices—were meant to awaken the darkness that

Silas bound himself to all those years ago. Claire's trying to finish what he started. She's trying to open the door he couldn't."

Mallory rolled her eyes. "Seriously? All of you believe in this bullshit?"

Darla laughed. "Still a skeptic? I suppose you don't trust your own senses. I know you saw it—the red glow. And didn't you feel the ground tremble with our power?"

"Whatever," Mallory replied. "What I believe isn't important. Obviously, you and the other cult freaks believe it, so why are you trying to open the door now?"

"Because the stars are aligning," Darla whispered. "The veil between worlds is thinning. With the right blood—*Bennington* blood—Claire can bring the darkness into this world permanently. And once it's here... once it steps through, nothing can stop it. *Nothing*. Not even you."

Garret rubbed his jaw. "How does she plan to do it? And why the women? What's their role in all of this?"

"They were simply vessels. Women from other branches of the Bennington bloodline. The darkness feeds on fear, pain, and despair, so the women were chosen for their lineage—to amplify the power of the ritual. Of course, we need more power, and there's another bloodline that's the key to all of this."

Garret leaned forward. "What bloodline? Whose blood is the key?"

Darla's lips curled into an enigmatic smirk, her eyes glittering with mockery. "Wouldn't you like to know?"

Mallory stood up and paced before turning back to Darla. "You've already told us a lot, Darla. If you really believe all this bullshit, why are you talking to us?"

Darla chuckled. "I've already told you. It doesn't matter what I tell you or what you do; you can't stop what's coming. Besides, doling out little chunks of information and seeing you scramble around, trying to figure it all out... it's fun."

Mallory sat back down and gripped the edge of the table. "What else do you know about Claire? Who helped her? Where will she go now?"

Darla's lips twitched, but she remained silent. After what felt like an eternity, she spoke again. "Claire has followers everywhere. People who will do anything for her. But the Maynard place, the old house—it was just the beginning. You'd be wise to look into her past. There are things she's kept hidden. Things even we didn't know about."

"What kind of things?" Mallory asked.

Darla shrugged nonchalantly. "I don't know everything, and even if I did, I wouldn't tell you. That would spoil the fun. But I'll give you a hint." She paused for a moment, as if relishing the suspense. "Look into her parents."

"Who's been feeding you information, Darla?" Garret's asked, his eyes narrowing. "Is it someone on my staff?"

Darla leaned back in her chair and let out a soft, mocking laugh. "Now why would I tell you that?"

Garret slammed his hand down onto the table with a force that made the metal echo, sending a sharp jolt through the room. "I'm tired of your games, Darla," he growled. "Tell me. Now."

Darla's eyes flicked to his, her smirk faltering for just a split second before she rolled her eyes dramatically. "Oh well, what do I care?" she muttered. Then, with a casual shrug, she said, "It's Ben Stockard... he's my nephew."

Mallory's eyes narrowed, and she stood up again. "I'm done with this conversation, but just so you know, Darla, I'll find Claire, and I *will* stop her. You can mark my words on that."

Garret gave a sharp nod of agreement, his eyes hardening as he stood to follow Mallory toward the door. Just then, Mallory's phone rang. Her pulse quickened as she glanced down at the screen and saw the name flashing across it. As she stepped out into the hallway, she answered quickly. "Hey, Mom. Now isn't a good time. Can I call you back?"

On the other end, there was only a thick, oppressive silence. Mallory frowned, pulling the phone back slightly, unsure if the call had connected properly.

"Mom?" she asked. "Mom, are you there?"

For a long, agonizing second, the silence stretched on. Then, suddenly, the phone crackled, and a low, eerie laugh echoed through the speaker. It wasn't her mother's voice.

"I've got your mom, Mallory," the voice hissed. "Your move."

The laugh returned, this time louder, sharper, like a knife scraping against her nerves. Mallory's heart slammed in her chest, and her grip tightened on the phone.

"WE HAVE TO FIND HER," Mallory snapped as she pushed through the door to the conference room.

"Hey, we'll find her," Garrett said, putting a hand on Mallory's shoulder.

"I ignored her for all those years, and now that we have a relationship again... what if..." Mallory whispered.

"She's gonna be okay. We'll find her."

Josie, sitting at the far end of the room, looked up as Mallory entered. Her eyes flickered briefly to Garret and then immediately to Mallory. "How'd it go?" she asked. Then, noticing Mallory's pallor, Josie's voice softened. "What's wrong?"

Mallory's jaw clenched, and the words fell from her mouth like a weight she could no longer carry. "Claire has my mom. We have to find them. There's no telling what she'll do to her." Mallory's voice broke on the last word.

Josie stood up, her chair scraping against the tile as she did. "What's the plan? "We can't waste time. Claire's too dangerous."

Mallory took a breath and forced her mind to work through the panic that threatened to cloud her thinking. "We need information. I want everything we have on Claire—her past, her family, anything. We need to know what drives her, who she's been working with, and where she might have taken my mom. If we find a trail, we can follow it."

Garret nodded and immediately went to his laptop. "Josie, I need you to focus on her associates. Ryan, help her out. She's not just recruiting random people. We need to find out who's been helping her."

Josie nodded and moved quickly to another terminal, her fingers flying across the keyboard as she began sorting through the data.

"While y'all do that, I'm going back through Claire's file," Mallory said. "I feel like there's something about her upbringing we're missing."

Garret glanced at her, his expression worried. "Trust your gut. That's a good place to start."

Mallory gave him a tight nod and took a seat at one of the side desks, pulling up Claire's file. As she scanned the documents, her fingers lingered over certain pieces—records from her time in the system, notes on Claire's behavior, but something didn't sit right.

"Here," Mallory murmured under her breath. "Claire's adoption records. A couple from Massachusetts adopted her. They were from out of state, nowhere near Blackwater Ridge. Her adoptive parents, John and Mary Reynolds, are deceased. I can't believe I missed this. They died when Claire was sixteen."

Josie turned toward Mallory. "What happened to them?"

"Hold up. Let me look it up." After a few moments, she pulled up an article detailing their deaths. "This says John Reynolds died in a car accident. The article says it was a freak accident, but rumors suggested it wasn't an accident at all. Mary Reynolds died shortly after. Authorities called it suicide."

Josie stood up from her desk and walked over to where Mallory was seated. "Whoa. That's pretty fishy."

"Where'd you say Claire's adoptive parents lived?" Garrett asked.

"Um," Mallory replied, looking for the town. "New Bedford, Massachusetts."

"Silas Bennington was from Massachusetts," Garret said. "It wasn't New Bedford, but hang on, let me see..." He typed furiously on his computer. "Silas Bennington came from a town called Gosnold. It's only twenty miles away from New Bedford."

Mallory's stomach turned. "There has to be a connection there—with Silas. Whatever happened to her parents... it's part of the story we're missing."

Josie's voice dropped as she looked at Mallory. "What if Claire had something to do with her parent's deaths?"

Before Mallory could respond, Garret called out, "I found something."

Mallory turned quickly and walked over to Garret's desk as he zoomed in on a map. "What is it?" she asked.

Garrett pointed to a section of the map. "This is the property Claire owns now, but it used to belong to Silas. See that little line right there? I didn't notice it before, but when I compared it to a map of an area I know well, I realized that line is a path. But look—" he traced his finger along the map, stopping at a point. "The path just ends. And here," he moved his finger further west, "there's a cave, perfectly in line with where the path stops. I'd be willing to bet everything there's a tunnel connecting the two."

"That's it," Mallory said. "That's where she's taking my mom. We need to go there. Now."

"I'll get the team ready," Josie said. "We'll head out right away."

IRIS SLOWLY OPENED her eyes, the dark, oppressive air surrounding her sending a chill down her spine. Only dim light filtered through the gloom, so she couldn't make out much, but her instincts told her she was either in a cellar or some forgotten cave deep underground.

Her heart raced as she tried to move and realized something was holding her in place. Her wrists were bound tightly to an unseen object. Panic bubbled up inside her, her breath quickening, when suddenly, a soft rustle broke the silence.

Iris froze. A figure moved ahead of her, shrouded in the shadows. Before she could react, a cruel, high-pitched laugh echoed through the space—an eerie, bone-chilling sound that seemed to reverberate in her bones.

"Oh, Iris," the voice sneered. "You're stuck here with me now. My plan is working perfectly."

The figure stepped into the dim light, revealing a young woman. She looked strangely familiar, yet Iris couldn't place her. The woman's eyes shimmered with a malevolent gleam.

"Who are you?" Iris asked, her voice trembling. "What do you want from me?"

The young woman let out a dark laugh. "Oh, silly woman," she said, her tone dripping with malice. "I don't want anything from you. I want your daughter. I *need* her. You see, she's the one who was prophesied—the one who will bring the Darkness back. *She* will be the final sacrifice. With her, the door to the Darkness will open once more."

Iris' blood ran cold at the woman's words. "No," she gasped, her eyes widening in disbelief and terror. "You can't—*she'll* stop you."

The young woman's smile twisted into something even more cruel and evil. "No, Iris," she purred. "Tonight is the night Mallory Crane dies."

Chapter Twenty

The night was unnervingly dark, far darker than a typical evening in Blackwater Ridge. The sky, thick with clouds, swallowed the light, leaving only shadows in its wake. Mallory gripped the steering wheel tightly as she pushed her SUV faster down the highway, the headlights barely cutting through the blackness ahead. Garret, Josie, and Ryan were with her, their faces tense with anticipation.

Behind them, the second SUV followed, carrying Agents Logan Archer, Elizabeth Morgan, and Sarah Kim. Sarah had flown in as soon as she received the news about Mallory's mom.

The realization of where Claire had taken Iris had come like a punch to the gut—back to the old Bennington farm. The abandoned property had long since fallen into disrepair, a place steeped in dark memories and even darker secrets. Once they'd made the connection, the team knew they needed to act quickly, but securing the warrant for the search wasn't simple. It had taken a flood of calls, pulling in favors and leaning on old connections. Two long, agonizing hours passed as Mallory waited for her boss, Agent Larkin, to work the channels and push the warrant through.

When they got close to the house, Mallory pulled out her radio. "Everyone stay alert," she said. "We have no idea what we're walking into here, so don't take anything for granted. We believe there is a tunnel beneath the house that leads to a hidden cave underground. If we're right, then that's where Claire has my mom, and I believe that's where everything is supposed to go down."

"Roger that," came Logan's voice through the radio.

At the Bennington Homeplace, they stepped out into the cold, damp air. Mallory took a deep breath and pulled out the crumpled map. She scanned the paper, then pointed toward the back of the property.

"Sarah, Logan, Lizzie," she instructed, "I need you three to follow this path toward the back of the property. There's a chance you'll be able to access the hidden room from up above. Take extra precautions. The layout is convoluted, and we don't know what we're dealing with inside."

Logan gave a nod, his face grim. "Understood."

Mallory turned to Garrett, Josie, and Ryan. "The four of us will head down to the cellar. If that tunnel leads to the cave, there's a good chance it also connects to the house. And my gut is telling me we'll find something down there. Keep your eyes peeled for anything that seems out of place."

Garret placed a hand on the grip of his weapon. "We'll find it."

With the plan set, the team split into two groups. Mallory led the way down the overgrown path toward the cellar. They reached the cellar door—rusted, creaking, and half-sunk into the ground. Mallory bent down and tested the handle, wincing as it squeaked in protest. After a moment's hesitation, she pushed it open. A gust of stale, cold air rushed out, making her shiver involuntarily. With a steady breath, she signaled for the others to follow her.

Inside, the cellar was a maze of old wooden beams and forgotten crates, the space far darker than Mallory had anticipated. Her flashlight beam sliced through the thick shadows, revealing an old furnace, piles of debris, and the faint outline of the stone floor. The space was eerily quiet, save for the distant sound of dripping water.

"This place has been untouched for years," Josie muttered, stepping carefully over a pile of broken wood. "Doesn't feel right."

Mallory nodded, her heart thudding in her chest. She moved cautiously forward, scanning every corner. "We need to find the tunnel."

They searched the area methodically, peeling back the layers of dust and debris. Garret pulled aside a stack of old crates, revealing a section of the floor that appeared older and more worn than the rest. He bent down, tapping the stone lightly with his knuckles.

"It's hollow," Garret said as he traced his fingers along the edge of the stone.

"Are you sure?" Mallory asked, moving closer to inspect.

"Yeah," Garret confirmed. "This isn't natural. There's something beneath this. Ryan, grab the crowbar."

Ryan moved quickly, his muscles straining as he wedged the crowbar into the cracks between the stones. The floor groaned before finally giving way with a loud scraping sound.

"Got it," Ryan said, wiping his forehead as the last of the stones shifted aside.

Beneath the floor, a narrow tunnel opened up. The walls were made of rough-hewn stone, and the air that wafted up was thick and musty, tinged with the scent of earth.

"I knew it," Mallory whispered. "This might be the tunnel Claire used to take my mom."

Garret stepped into the opening, his flashlight illuminating the path ahead. "We'll have to move fast. She could be anywhere by now. Y'all go ahead while I radio the rest of the team. I'll be right behind you."

Josie and Ryan nodded in agreement, and together, they made their way into the tunnel.

"Stay close," Mallory ordered.

After what felt like an eternity, they reached a dead end. The tunnel narrowed, with a pile of broken stone and rubble blocking their path. Mallory's heart sank.

"Great," Ryan muttered, kicking at the debris. "It's blocked."

Garret didn't look discouraged. He crouched down, examining the rubble more closely. "It's not blocked. This is a door."

Mallory frowned, stepping closer. "What do you mean? It's just debris."

"Look at the edges," Garret said, tapping his flashlight on the stone. "This isn't natural. Someone designed it to resemble a random pile of rocks, but it's actually a door—probably meant to throw anyone off who might stumble across it.

Mallory's breath caught in her throat. "You think Claire expected someone to find this?"

"It's possible," Garret replied, his expression unreadable as he pushed against the stone. After a moment, the door creaked open with a low groan.

The passage beyond was narrow, with musty air and slick floors, but Mallory didn't hesitate. She stepped forward, her mind focused on finding her mother and stopping Claire.

Meanwhile, Logan's team had been searching the woods around the property, checking for signs of hidden access points to the tunnel. Sarah, Logan, and Lizzie had split up to cover more ground, but despite their best efforts, they hadn't found anything useful—until Lizzie stumbled across a small, rusted hatch hidden beneath a large bush near the ridge.

"This looks like something," Lizzie said, brushing the limbs away from the edges of the hatch. She pulled at it, but it wouldn't budge.

Logan stepped in, his strength enough to pry the hatch open. "Down we go,"

THE UNDERGROUND CAVE loomed ominously before Mallory and her team. Its jagged walls, slick with moisture, stretched upward like the darkened spine of some ancient, forgotten beast.

Mallory's heart pounded. She was close. She could feel it. Her mother was down there—somewhere in the dark. "Stay alert, guys. We don't know what we're about to walk into," Mallory whispered.

"Always," Josie replied.

The sounds of dripping water and distant creaks echoed in the vast, underground space as they moved deeper into the cave. Mallory's pulse quickened as they entered a large chamber. Her flashlight swept over the area, illuminating a massive altar at the far end of the cave. Surrounding it, a dozen candles burned, casting flickering shadows that seemed to writhe with an unnatural energy. Symbols—strange, glowing, and foreign—were etched into the stone floor, their lines shifting like they were alive.

Claire stood in the center of the altar, draped in a black robe, her face illuminated by the eerie candlelight. Her hands were raised above her head, holding a jagged, ceremonial dagger, its blade covered in strange markings, glowing with a faint but unsettling light.

Beside the altar, Iris was kneeling. She looked weak, her face pale, but her eyes locked onto Mallory's with a desperate, pleading expression. A breath of relief surged through Mallory's chest—her mother was alive—but the sight of her held captive, surrounded by this unholy ritual, threatened to tear the breath from her lungs.

"You're too late," Claire's voice rang out. Her eyes, now glowing faintly, locked onto Mallory's. "The darkness is already here. The world will fall, and I will be its queen."

Mallory didn't hesitate. Raising her weapon, she stepped forward, keeping her eyes fixed on Claire. "Let her go, Claire. This ends now. Step away from the altar."

Claire's twisted grin deepened as she lowered the dagger. "You think you can stop me? I have already opened the gate. The darkness will take this world, and nothing you do can stop it. You, Mallory... you are the key to it all."

"I'm not key to shit," Mallory growled.

Behind her, Josie shifted. "What now?" she asked.

"We stop her. We have to." Mallory replied. "Whatever it takes."

As Mallory prepared to advance, a sound from above caught her attention—footsteps. Echoing down into the cavern, the sound of their backup had arrived.

Logan, Sarah, and Lizzy came in from above the chamber, their movement precise and coordinated as they navigated the complex system of narrow tunnels leading to the cavern. Each of them had their weapon drawn, ready for whatever came next.

The team was finally complete.

"Claire Crawford," Logan called out, his voice steady, authoritative. "You're under arrest. Step away from the altar and surrender."

Claire's laughter echoed through the cave, hollow and chilling. "You still don't understand, do you?" Her voice dropped to something dangerous and ethereal. "This isn't about me. It's about destiny. The darkness chose me. The darkness will win."

"And we're here to make sure that doesn't happen," Sarah said.

The ground beneath them trembled, and the air filled with a low, rumbling hum. The symbols on the floor glowed brighter, flickering like fire.

Claire raised her dagger high, her voice rising in a chant that Mallory couldn't understand. The candles around the altar flared, casting long, twisting shadows that swirled in unnatural patterns.

Suddenly, a gust of cold wind blew through the cave, extinguishing most of the candles, but the symbols on the ground burned brighter still, lighting the entire cavern with a sickly glow. The ground beneath them shook violently, throwing Mallory and Josie off-balance. Then, the shadows surrounding the altar merged into something much more sinister—an enormous, formless mass of shifting darkness. Eyes, thousands of eyes, opened inside the shadow, blinking and staring with malevolent intent.

"Holy shit. Is that what she's summoning?" Ryan whispered.

Mallory's eyes never left Claire. "I don't know, but we need to stop her. Now."

Suddenly, Claire's voice turned into a scream, her body lurching forward with unnatural speed. She lunged toward Mallory, the ceremonial dagger held high.

"Move!" Garret shouted.

But it was too late. Claire's blade descended toward Mallory's chest.

Garret reacted first, tackling Claire to the ground just as the dagger grazed Mallory's shoulder. Mallory stumbled back, gasping for air, her blood already soaking through her shirt. She barely had time to register the pain when Garret and Claire collided in a struggle for control of the blade.

"Shoot her! Shoot the altar," Mallory shouted, trying to steady herself.

Ryan, Josie, Logan, Sarah, and Elizabeth reacted instantly. They aimed their weapons at the altar, firing shot after shot, but the bullets had no effect.

"Keep it up!" Logan barked. "I don't know what the hell this is, but we need to break the connection!"

The shadows around them grew, with tendrils of darkness stretching out to the far corners of the cavern. The massive, shadowy entity above the altar grew larger, swirling and writhing.

Mallory's mind raced. There had to be something to stop this.

"Mom," Mallory shouted, her voice cracking with urgency. "Look at me!"

Iris' eyes fluttered, and for a brief moment, they locked onto Mallory's. "The ritual... the symbols... disrupt them... Mallory..."

"Disrupt the symbols?" Mallory repeated, her heart hammering in her chest. She glanced at Garret, who was still wrestling with Claire on the ground.

"I've got this," Garret growled, pushing Claire back as the woman howled in rage.

Mallory's eyes scanned the ground. The glowing symbols—they formed a pattern, but how could she disrupt them?

"There," Mallory shouted as she spotted a loose stone on the floor beside the altar. "Grab the stone!"

Without hesitation, Logan rushed forward and threw the stone onto one of the glowing symbols. As it struck, the ground trembled, and the dark shadow above the altar shrieked, its form cracking and destabilizing.

Claire's voice rose in fury. "No!" She scrambled toward the altar, but the energy was fading. The shadow began to collapse.

Logan kicked the stone into place, forcing the runes to crack and splinter. The shadow let out a deafening scream, disintegrating in a sudden burst of light. The candles flickered out, and the ground beneath them quit shaking.

Claire staggered back, her eyes wide with horror. In a final, desperate attempt, she lunged once more for Mallory, but before she could strike, Josie tackled her from behind. Claire struggled against her grip and finally broke free, shoving Josie hard against the cave wall.

Claire reached for the dagger, but Mallory stepped forward, breathing heavily, and swung her weapon toward Claire, striking her hard enough to knock her unconscious.

"Is it over?" Josie asked, wiping her brow and getting up.

Mallory looked at her mother, now slumped to the side, but alive. She felt a rush of relief that almost knocked the wind out of her.

"Yeah, it's over," Mallory breathed. "Josie, are you okay?"

"I'll be all right. Just some bruises. That bitch is strong," Josie replied.

As the team moved to secure Claire, Mallory knelt beside her mother, wrapping her arms around her tightly. "I've got you, Mom. We're safe."

Chapter Twenty-One

The crisp, cool autumn air carried the first hints of winter's approach, a reminder that the seasons were shifting in Blackwater Ridge. It had been two weeks since the final showdown at the Bennington farm, but the scars—both seen and unseen—remained.

Mallory sat on the front porch of her childhood home, cradling a lukewarm mug of coffee. She watched as the early morning light filtered through the bare trees, casting a soft, golden glow over the quiet street.

To Mallory, the town felt different now. Lighter. Friendlier. Happier. But in her heart, something was still missing. She couldn't feel the warmth yet—not fully. Maybe she never would. Only time would tell.

As the memories of the darkness played in her mind like a never-ending reel, Mallory couldn't escape the images. The screams. The confusion. The chaos. And Claire's eyes—the fear that had clouded them when she realized it was over, that she had been defeated. It hadn't felt like a triumph in that moment. It felt like a hollow sense of fate. The end of one chapter, and the uneasy beginning of another.

Just then, the front door creaked open. Mallory looked up to see her mother stepping out onto the porch, a blanket wrapped around her shoulders.

"You're up early," Iris said with a soft smile.

Mallory smiled back, her eyes tired. "Yeah, I haven't been able to sleep much lately. It's like my brain won't shut off."

Iris placed a gentle hand on Mallory's shoulder. "I can't even begin to imagine what you're going through. I was there, and I still can't believe what I saw. I don't think I'll ever fully recover from it. I know you've handled tough cases before, but this... this was personal. That's going to take longer to process."

Mallory gazed out at the mountain in the distance, a soft sigh escaping her lips. "You're right. Mom, when I got that phone call, that Claire had taken you... my whole world fell apart. I'm so grateful I was able to get you back."

Iris nodded. "I know, Sweetie. I'm thankful, too. But I get the feeling there's something else on your mind."

Mallory hesitated for a moment. "I'm struggling with what to do about the phone call I got yesterday."

Iris looked at her daughter with understanding eyes. "Like I said last night, *you* have to make that decision, Mallory. Nobody else can make it for you. But whatever you choose, you have my full support." She leaned down and kissed Mallory on the top of her head. "I'm going to head back inside to get ready for my lunch with Maggie. I've got some old documents I think she'd like to see."

Mallory watched as her mother walked back into the house. She felt a deep sense of gratitude for the way their relationship had begun to heal. They were talking more, understanding each other better, and the bond they once shared was slowly returning.

With a soft exhale, Mallory allowed herself a quiet moment. The weight of everything that had happened still lingered, but she could feel her thoughts settling, pushing the world around her into the background. She could finally breathe again—at least for now.

"Morning." The voice broke the silence, pulling Mallory from her thoughts.

She turned to see Garret standing at the bottom of the porch steps, holding a paper bag in one hand and two cups of coffee in the other. "I thought you might be up," he said, climbing the steps and handing her one of the mugs.

"Thanks," Mallory replied, taking the hot coffee and abandoning the now-cold cup on the table beside her. "You didn't have to do this."

"I wanted to," he said with a shrug as he settled into the chair next to her.

Boone padded over, tail wagging, and laid his head in Mallory's lap. "Good morning, Boone," she said, scratching him behind the ears. "Let me guess, bagels?" Mallory asked, her lips curving into a faint smile as she glanced at the bag.

"You're welcome. I know how much you love the bagels from the bakery on Main Street," Garret said, tossing Boone a small biscuit from his pocket. "I thought I'd bring you one and check in with you. We haven't had a chance to talk much lately. You've been distant, almost isolated, since..."

He didn't need to finish the sentence. They both knew what he meant—since Claire, the darkness, and everything that had happened.

Mallory sighed, taking a long sip of her coffee. "I've been processing it all," she said quietly.

Garret nodded, not pushing her. "Hey, you're allowed to take time to process, to sort through your feelings. No one expects you to have it all figured out overnight."

"I know," she murmured. "But I can't stop thinking about how it all played out. How Claire got pulled into all of this."

"Yeah, it's quite the story," Garrett said.

"But it wasn't just the darkness, Garrett. It was everything—years of pain, abandonment, isolation, resentment. That's what made her vulnerable." She exhaled sharply, shaking her head. "I should've caught it sooner. And I was so damn stubborn about refusing to believe in anything supernatural. I mean, I grew up being hounded about 'evil darkness' at every turn, and I resented it so much that I refused to even entertain the possibility. But that resentment—it compromised me. It made me blind. I shouldn't have missed the signs. I should've dug deeper into the backgrounds of all the women who went missing. I let my past dictate what I was willing to see, and because of that, I wasn't looking closely enough at the present. I know better than that—I'm a veteran agent, for God's sake."

"No," Garret said firmly, shaking his head. "You're not responsible for what happened—not for missing any signs that might have been there. We all missed those signs. I investigated her past, but I didn't think to go back further than a few years. I didn't think it was relevant." He paused, meeting her gaze. "So, if anyone is to blame, it's me. But you stopped it, Mallory. That's what matters. That's what's important."

Mallory didn't respond immediately. She let his words sink in, staring out at the street as the town slowly began to wake up.

"I received a call yesterday," Mallory said after a moment, her voice hesitant.

"Oh?" Garret raised an eyebrow, intrigued.

She nodded. "From the Bureau. Agent Ramirez. She's the regional supervisor for the area."

Garret's expression shifted to one of surprise and concern. "That sounds important."

"She offered me a new job," Mallory continued. "A chance to head up a task force focused on the Appalachia Mountain region. I'd be investigating specialized cases—things most people wouldn't even believe were real."

Garret let out a low whistle. "That's huge, Mallory. Your own team."

"Yeah," she replied, leaning back in her chair. "It's everything I've ever wanted—leading my own team, solving cases that matter, making a real difference. But there's a catch, and it's a big one."

"You'd have to be based out of Blackwater Ridge?" Garret guessed.

Mallory nodded slowly, her expression grave. "I'd have to move here. Permanently. And I'm not sure I can do that. This town, these mountains... they hold so much of my past. Moving here means confronting it all every day."

Garret considered her words for a moment before responding. "And leaving? How does that make you feel?"

"It feels like I'd be running," she admitted, her voice tinged with uncertainty. "But I'm not sure I'm strong enough to stay."

"Mallory, you're stronger than you think," Garret said. "You've proven that to me—*and* to this town. But no one can make this decision for you. You have to make it for yourself. Only you know what you need, what's best for your life."

"You sound like Iris," she replied with a smile. Then, she exhaled, her chest tight with the weight of the decision she was facing.

"Iris is a smart woman, and so are you. In the end, whatever you decide," Garret added, standing up and placing a hand on her shoulder, "just remember, you've already faced two of the worst things this town has to offer—Claire and the darkness. If you can survive that, you can survive anything."

Mallory looked up at him. "Thanks, Garret. I appreciate your support and kindness."

He grinned. "Anytime."

THE CAVE WAS COLDER than Mallory remembered, the chill more biting than it had been the last time she was here. The deeper she ventured, the darker it became. She hadn't been back since the night they'd found Susannah's old chest, and now, standing in the same spot, memories of that moment surged back, vivid and painful.

Her boots crunched on the rocky ground as she made her way toward the center of the cavern. The silence was unnerving, broken only by the faint, rhythmic drip of water that echoed in the stillness. Her pulse quickened—not from fear, but from the weight of the decision that had brought her here.

Mallory switched off her flashlight, plunging herself into complete darkness. She closed her eyes, allowing the silence to envelop her like a heavy blanket. Her thoughts wandered back to the stories from her childhood—stories of ghosts, curses, and things that lurked just beyond the veil of reality. She thought about Susannah Fairchild, the girl who had died here in 1894, her life cruelly snatched away by forces she could never escape.

"Susannah, I don't know if you can hear me," Mallory whispered, her voice trembling. "This is probably silly, but I thought maybe coming here would give me the answers to the questions that have been haunting me."

She folded her arms and leaned against the cool stone wall.

"You never had a choice. Your life was stolen from you in the cruelest way. Your daughter, Hope—she never had a choice either. She grew up without her mother and father. It isn't fair. Claire grew up the same way, without either of her parents. But Claire..."

Mallory's voice caught in her throat. She paused, taking a shaky breath.

"Claire chose this path, Susannah. She gave in to her pain, let it consume her, until there was nothing left. I'm afraid. Afraid that if I stay, if I face everything this place holds, I'll end up just as lost. Just as broken."

The only reply was the drip of water, but something in the darkness felt different. It felt... eager, as though the cave itself was alive, listening to her every word.

"I don't know. Maybe that's the point. Maybe I'm supposed to stay, not to run from the past, but to face it. To honor you, to honor Hope. To make sure this town remembers your lives so no one else becomes a tragic victim—or a *willing* villain, like Claire."

She stood there for a long moment, letting the weight of Susannah's memory settle over her. Then, it happened—a sudden, vision, like a flicker in the darkness. In the corner of her eye, Mallory saw the image of Susannah and Tobias, standing together, hand in hand, smiling. They were happy—free from pain, free from the past that had held them captive. The image was fleeting, but it filled Mallory's heart with something unexpected—a sense of peace.

A smile tugged at her lips, and she felt the answer seep into her heart like warm sunlight. The darkness of the cave, which had seemed to suffocate her moments before, now felt less oppressive, less suffused with danger. It was as if Susannah herself had offered her blessing.

"I'll stay in Blackwater Ridge," Mallory said softly, her words echoing off the stone walls. "I'll stay. I'll fight for this town. For its people. For those who still need someone to believe in them."

Epilogue

Two Months Later...

The new office wasn't much to look at. A small, hastily converted space above the Blackwater Ridge sheriff's station, it served as the headquarters for the newly formed Unusual Crimes Unit. Its location was convenient, with the sheriff's team just a staircase away, but the room itself left much to be desired. The walls were bare, the paint scuffed from years of neglect. Mismatched desks were arranged haphazardly, their surfaces still cluttered with remnants of the previous tenants. Yet, despite its shortcomings, it was a start—a blank slate for something greater.

Mallory Crane stood at the head of the room, her hands resting on the scratched surface of a table that had seen better days. Her sharp gaze swept across the space, taking in her newly assembled team. The weight of responsibility settled on her shoulders, but she stood tall, exuding the quiet confidence that had carried her through so much already.

In the corner, Garret Cole, Ryan Taylor, and Josie Rhodes stood as silent observers. They were there for moral support, each offering an encouraging nod as Mallory prepared to address the team.

The faces around the table were a mix of the familiar and the new. Tasha Reynolds, a former wildlife ranger turned FBI agent, sat closest to Mallory. Her reputation for tracking anything, anywhere, preceded her. Across from her, Owen Burke was already hunched over his laptop, his fingers flying across the keys. A tech-savvy analyst from D.C., Owen was the team's digital bloodhound, able to sift through mountains of data to uncover patterns others missed. Next to him sat Logan Archer and Sarah Kim, both of whom had worked with Mallory on her previous team and had proven themselves indispensable during the chaos that had unfolded in Blackwater Ridge months before.

Mallory took a steadying breath, her voice firm as she began. "This is it. The Unusual Crimes Unit. Our job is to take on cases no one else will touch—cases dismissed as hoaxes, urban legends, or unsolvable mysteries. It's up to us to uncover the truth, no matter how strange or dangerous it may seem."

Tasha raised an eyebrow, a skeptical smile tugging at her lips. "So, what are we hunting—ghosts? Bigfoot?"

Garret chuckled softly from his spot by the door, but Mallory's expression didn't waver. "If Bigfoot starts abducting hikers, then yes, we'll hunt him down," she said flatly.

The humor dissipated, and the team straightened in their chairs.

"We've already got our first case," Mallory continued, sliding a thick file across the table. "Two hikers went missing in Graves Hollow, just over the county line. Locals have reported strange lights in the woods, livestock mutilations, and…" She paused, her eyes scanning the report. "…something they call the 'Crying Child.'"

Owen frowned, glancing up from his laptop. "Isn't that just an urban legend? There are stories about a crying child in woods all over the place."

"Maybe," Mallory acknowledged. "But legends usually start with a sliver of truth. It's our job to figure out what's real and what isn't. Those hikers didn't just vanish into thin air."

Garret leaned against the doorframe as he listened. "Sounds like you're diving into the deep end right out of the gate."

"Would you expect anything less?" Mallory replied with a faint smile.

The team began poring over the case file, their voices blending as they strategized and assigned tasks. Tasha examined topographic maps, pointing out trails and potential search areas. Owen scoured satellite images and scouted for patterns in local reports, while Logan and Sarah outlined communication protocols and contingency plans.

Mallory stepped back, letting them settle into their rhythm. She watched as they worked, a quiet sense of pride blooming in her chest. For the first time in a long time, she felt a spark of purpose—a purpose that extended beyond the shadow of her own past and the darkness that had plagued Blackwater Ridge.

Her gaze drifted to the window, where the vast expanse of the Appalachian Mountains stretched into the horizon, their peaks shrouded in mist. A chill ran down her spine, not from fear but from the certainty that this was only the beginning. The mountains were old, older than memory, and they held secrets darker than anyone dared to imagine.

A flicker of movement caught her eye. For a brief, haunting moment, she thought she saw two figures standing on the ridgeline—ghostly and shimmering in the distance. Susannah and Tobias, hand in hand, their faces calm and content. The vision lingered just long enough to fill Mallory with a strange sense of peace before it dissolved into the swirling mist.

Turning back to her team, she cleared her throat, her voice commanding their attention. "Alright, everyone. Let's get to work. Let's find these hikers before it's too late."